THE WHIT. RABIL

A N D   O T H E R   S T O R I E S

BY CLARK ASHTON SMITH

The Double Shadow
The Maker of Gargoyles and Other Stories
The Best of Clark Ashton Smith (forthcoming)

THE WHITE SYBIL
AND OTHER STORIES

CLARK ASHTON SMITH

WILDSIDE PRESS

THE WHITE SYBIL AND OTHER STORIES

"The White Sybil" originally appeared as a booklet in 1934 from Fantasy Publications. "Chinoiserie" originally appeared in *The Philippine Magazine*, November 1931. "The Raja and the Tiger" originally appeared in *The Black Cat*, February 1912. "The Justice of the Elephant" originally appeared in *Oriental Stories*, Autumn 1931. "The Kiss of Zoraida" originally appeared in *The Magic Carpet Magazine*, July 1933. "The Ghoul" originally appeared in *The Fantasy Fan*, January 1934. "Something New" originally appeared in *10 Story Book*, August 1924. "The Malay Krise" originally appeared in *The Overland Monthly*, October 1910. "The Ghost of Mohammed Din" originally appeared in *The Overland Monthly*, November 1910. "The Mirror in the Hall of Ebony" originally appeared in *The Fantasy Fan*, May 1934. "The Mahout" originally appeared in *The Black Cat*, August 1911. "The Primal City" originally appeared in *The Fantasy Fan*, November 1934. "The Passing of Aphrodite" originally appeared in *The Fantasy Fan*, December 1934. "The Tale of Sir John Maundeville" originally appeared in *The Fantasy Fan*, October 1933 (as "The Kingdom of the Worm"). "The Hunters from Beyond" originally appeared in *Strange Tales*, October 1932. "The Light from Beyond" originally appeared in *Wonder Stories*, April 1933.

For more information, contact:

Wildside Press
www.wildsidepress.com

CONTENTS

THE WHITE SYBIL

TORTHA, the poet, with strange austral songs in his heart, and the umber of high and heavy suns on his face, had come back to his native city of Cerngoth, in Mhu Thulan, by the Hyperborean sea. Far had he wandered in the quest of that alien beauty which had fled always before him like the horizon. Beyond Commoriom of the white, numberless spires, and beyond the marsh-grown jungles to the south of Commoriom, he had floated on nameless rivers, and had crossed the half-legendary realm of Tscho Vulpanomi, upon whose diamond-sanded, ruby-graveled shore an ignescent ocean was said to beat forever with fiery spume.

He had beheld many marvels, and things incredible to relate: the uncouthly carven gods of the South, to whom blood was spilt on sun-approaching towers; the plumes of the *huusim*, which were many yards in length and were colored like pure flame; the mailed monsters of the austral swamps; the proud argosies of Mu and Antillia, which moved by enchantment, without oar or sail; the fuming peaks that were shaken perpetually by the struggles of imprisoned demons. But, walking at noon on the streets of Cerngoth, he met a stranger marvel than these. Idly, with no expectation of other than homely things, he beheld the White Sybil of Polarion.

He knew not whence she had come, but suddenly she was before him in the throng. Amid the tawny girls of Cerngoth with their russet hair and blue-black eyes, she was like an apparition descended from the moon. Goddess, ghost or woman, he knew not which, she passed fleetly and was gone: a creature of snow and norland light, with eyes like moon-pervaded pools, and lips that were smitten with the same pallor as the brow and bosom. Her gown was of some filmy white fabric, pure and ethereal as her person.

In wonder that turned to startled rapture, Tortha gazed at the miraculous being, and sustained for a moment the strangely thrilling light of her chill eyes, in which he seemed to find an obscure recognition, such as a long-veiled divinity, appearing at last, would vouchsafe to her worshipper.

Somehow, she seemed to bring with her the infrangible solitude of remote places, the death-deep hush of lonely plateaus and mountains. A silence, such as might dwell in some abandoned city, fell on the chaffering, chattering crowd as she went by; and the people drew back from her in sudden awe. Before the silence could break into gossiping murmurs, Tortha had guessed her identity.

He knew that he had seen the White Sybil, that mysterious being who was rumored to come and go as if by some preterhuman agency in the cities of Hyperborea. No man had ever learned her name, or her nativity; but she was said to descend like a spirit from the bleak mountains to the north of Cerngoth; from the desert land of Polarion, where the oncoming glaciers crept in valleys that had once been fertile with fern and cycad, and passes that had been the highways of busy traffic.

No one had ever dared to accost or follow her. Often she came and went in silence; but sometimes, in the marts or public squares, she would utter cryptic prophecies and tidings of doom. In many places, throughout Mhu Thulan and central Hyperborea, she had foretold the enormous sheet of ice, now crawling gradually downward from the pole, that would cover the continent in ages to come, and would bury beneath oblivious drift the mammoth palms of its jungles and the superb pinnacles of its cities. And in great Commoriom, then the capital, she had prophesied a stranger doom that was to befall this city long before the encroachment of the ice. Men feared her everywhere, as a messenger of unknown outland gods, moving abroad in supernal bale and beauty.

All this, Tortha had heard many times; and he had wondered somewhat at the tale, but had soon dismissed it from his mind, being laden with marvelous memories of exotic things. But now that he had seen the Sybil, it was as if an unexpected revelation had been offered to him; as if he had discerned, briefly and afar, the hidden goal of a mystic pilgrimage.

In that single glimpse, he had found the personification of all the vague ideals and unfixed longings that had drawn him from land to land. Here was the eluding strangeness he had sought on alien breasts and waters, and beyond horizons of fire-vomiting mountains. Here was the veiled Star, whose name and luster he had never known. The moon-cold eyes of the Sybil had kindled a strange love in Tortha, to whom love had been, at most, no more than a passing agitation of the senses.

However, on that occasion, it did not occur to him that he might follow the visitant or come to learn more concerning her. Momentarily, he was content with the rare vision that had fired his soul and dazzled his senses. Dreaming such dreams as the moon might inspire in a moth; dreams through which the Sybil moved like a woman-shaped flame on ways too far and too steep for human feet, he returned to his house in Cerngoth.

The days that ensued were dim and dreamlike to Tortha, and were presided over by his memory of the white apparition. A mad Uranian fever mounted in his soul, together with the sure knowledge that he sought an impossible fruition. Idly, to beguile the hours, he copied the poems he had written during his journey, or turned over the pages of boyish manuscripts. All were equally void and without meaning now, like the sere leaves of a bygone year.

With no prompting on the part of Tortha, his servants and visitors spoke to him of the Sybil. Seldom, they said, had she entered Cerngoth, appearing more often in cities remote from the ice-bound waste of Polarion. Truly, she was no mortal being, for she had been seen on the same day in places hundreds of miles apart. Huntsmen had sometimes met her on the mountains above Cerngoth; but always, when encountered thus, she had disappeared quickly, like a morning vapor that melts among the crags.

The poet, listening with a moody and absent mien, spoke of his love to no one. He knew well that his kinsfolk and acquaintances would think this passion a more errant madness than the youthful yearning that had led him to unheard-of lands. No human lover had aspired to the Sybil, whose beauty was a perilous brightness, akin to meteor and fireball; a fatal and lethal beauty, born of transarctic gulfs, and somehow one with the far doom of worlds.

Like the brand of frost or flame, her memory burned in Tortha. Musing among his neglected books, or walking abroad in reverie on which no outward thing could intrude, he saw always before him the pale radiance of the Sybil. He seemed to hear a whisper from boreal solitudes: a murmur of ethereal sweetness, sharp as ice-born air, vocal with high, unearthly words, that sang of inviolate horizons and the chill glory of lunar auroras above continents impregnable to man.

The long summer days went by, bringing the outland folk to trade their furs and eider in Cerngoth, and damaskeening the slopes beyond the city with flowers of bright azure and vermilion. But the Sybil was not seen again in Cerngoth, nor was she heard of in other cities. It seemed as if her visitations had ceased; as if, having delivered the tidings committed to her by the outer gods, she would appear no more in the haunts of mankind.

Amid the despair that was twin to his passion, Tortha had nurtured a hope that he might again behold the visitant. Slowly the hope grew fainter; but left his longing undiminished. In his daily walks he now went farther afield, leaving the houses and streets and turning toward the mountains that glowered above Cerngoth, guarding with icy horns the glacier-taken plateau of Polarion.

Higher he went each day on the hills, lifting his eyes to the dark crags from which the Sybil was rumored to descend. An obscure message seemed to call him on; and still, for a time, he did not dare to obey the summons wholly, but turned back to Cerngoth.

There came the forenoon when he climbed to a hill-meadow from which the roofs of the city were like littered shells beside a sea whose tumbling billows had become a smooth floor of turquoise. He was alone in a world of flowers: the frail mantle that summer had flung before the desolate peaks. The turf rolled away from him on every hand in broad scrolls and carpetries of flaming color. Even the wild briars had put forth their fragile, sanguine-tinted blossoms; and the very banks and precipices were heavily arrassed with low-hanging bloom.

Tortha had met no one; for he had long since left the trail by which the squat mountain people came to the city. A vague prompting, which seemed to include a promise unspoken by any voice, had led him to this lofty meadow from which a crystal rill ran seaward amid the bright cascades of flowers.

Pale, diaphanous beneath the sun, a few cirrus clouds went floating idly toward the pinnacles; and the quarrying hawks flew oceanward on broad red wings. A perfume, rich as temple-incense, rose from the blossoms whereon he had trampled; the light lay still and heavy upon him, dazzling his senses; and Tortha, a little weary from his climbing, grew faint for a moment with some strange vertigo.

Recovering, he saw before him the White Sybil, who stood amid the flowers of blood-red and cerulean like a goddess of the snow attired in veils of moon-flame. Her pale eyes, pouring an icy rapture into his veins, regarded him enigmatically. With a gesture of her hand that was like the glimmering of light on inaccessible places, she beckoned him to follow, as she turned and went upward along the slope above the meadow.

Tortha had forgotten his fatigue; had forgotten all but the celestial beauty of the Sybil. He did not question the enchantment that claimed him, the wild Uranian ecstasy that rose in his heart. He knew only that she had reappeared to him, had beckoned him; and he followed.

Soon the hills grew steeper against the overtowering crags; and barren ribs of rock emerged gloomily through the mantling flowerage. Without effort, light as a drifting vapor, the Sybil climbed on before Tortha. He could not approach her; and though the interval of distance between then increased at times, he did not altogether lose sight of her luminous figure.

Now he was among bleak ravines and savage scarps, where the Sybil was like a swimming star in the chasmal, crag-flung shadows. The fierce mountain eagles screamed above him, eyeing his progress as they flew about their eyries. The chill trickle of rills born of the eternal glaciers fell upon him from overbeetling ledges; and sudden chasms yawned before his feet with a hollow roaring of vertiginous waters far below.

Tortha was conscious only of an emotion such as impels the moth to pursue a wandering flame. He did not picture to himself the aim and end of his pursuit, nor the fruition of the weird love that drew him on. Oblivious of mortal fatigue, of peril and disaster that might lie before him, he felt the delirium of a mad ascent to superhuman heights.

Above the wild ravines and escarpments, he came to a lofty pass that had led formerly between Mhu Thulan and Polarion. Here an olden highway, creviced and chasmed, and partly blocked with debris of avalanches and fallen watchtowers, ran between walls of winter-eaten rock. Down the pass, like some enormous dragon of glittering ice, there poured the vanguard of the boreal glaciers to meet the Sybil and Tortha.

Amid the strange ardor of his ascent, the poet was aware of a sudden chill that had touched the noontide. The rays of the sun had grown dull and heatless; the shadows were like the depth of ice-hewn Arctic tombs. A film of ochreous cloud, moving with magical swiftness, swept athwart the day and darkened like a dusty web, till the sun glowed through it lifeless and pale as a moon in December. The heavens above and beyond the pass were closed in with curtains of leaden-threaded grey.

Into the gathering dimness, over the glacier's machicolated ice, the Sybil sped like a flying fire, paler and more luminous against the somber cloud.

Now Tortha had climbed the fretted incline of the ice that crawled out from Polarion. He had gained the summit of the pass and would soon reach the open plateau beyond. But like a storm raised up by preterhuman sorcery, the snow was upon him now in spectral swirls and blinding flurries. It came as with the ceaseless flight of soft wide wings, the measureless coiling of vague and pallid dragons.

For a time he still discerned the Sybil, as one sees the dim glowing of a sacred lamp through altar-curtains that descend in some great temple. Then the snow thickened, till he no longer saw the guiding gleam, and knew not if he still wandered through the walled pass, or was lost upon some bournless plain of perpetual winter.

He fought for breath in the storm-stifled air. The clear white fire that had sustained him seemed to sink and fall in his icy limbs. The unearthly fervor and exaltation died away, leaving a dark fatigue, an ever-spreading numbness that rose through all his being. The bright image of the Sybil was no more than a nameless star that fell with all else he had ever known or dreamed into grey forgetfulness. . . .

Tortha opened his eyes to a strange world. Whether he had fallen and had died in the storm, or had stumbled on somehow through its white oblivion, he could not guess: but around him now there was no trace of the driving snow or the glacier-shackled mountains.

He stood in a valley that might have been the inmost heart of some boreal paradise — a valley that was surely no part of waste Polarion. About him the turf was piled with flowers that had the frail and pallid hues of a lunar rainbow. Their delicate forms were those of the blossoms of snow and frost, and it seemed that they would melt and vanish at a touch.

The sky above the valley was not the low-arching, tender turquoise heaven of Mhu Thulan, but was vague, dreamlike, remote, and full of an infinite violescence, like the welkin of a world beyond time and space. Everywhere there was light; but Tortha saw no sun in the cloudless vault. It was as if the sun, the moon, the stars, had been molten together ages ago and had dissolved into some ultimate, eternal luminescence.

Tall, slender trees, whose leafage of lunar green was thickly starred with blossoms delicate as those of the turf, grew in groves and clumps above the valley, and lined the margin of a stilly flowing stream that wound away into measureless misty perspectives.

Tortha noticed that he cast no shadow on the flowered ground. The trees likewise were shadowless, and
were not reflected in the clear still waters. No wind lifted
the blossom-heavy boughs, or stirred the countless petals
amid the grass. A cryptic silence brooded over all things,
like the hush of some supernal doom.

Filled with a high wonder, but powerless to surmise
the riddle of his situation, the poet turned as if at the bidding of an imperatory voice. Behind him, and near at
hand, there was an arbor of flowering vines that had
draped themselves from tree to tree. Through the half-
parted arras of bloom, in the bower's heart, he saw like a
drifted snow the white veils of the Sybil.

With timid steps, with eyes that faltered before her
mystic beauty, and a flaming as of blown torches in his
heart, he entered the arbor. From the bank of blossoms on
which she reclined, the Sybil rose to receive her worshipper. . . .

Of all that followed, much was forgotten afterwards
by Tortha. It was like a light too radiant to be endured,
a thought that eluded conception through surpassing
strangeness. It was real beyond all that men deem reality:
and yet it seemed to Tortha that he, the Sybil, and all that
surrounded them, were part of an after-mirage on the
deserts of time; that he was poised insecurely above life
and death in some bright, fragile bower of dreams.

He thought that the Sybil greeted him in thrilling,
mellifluous words of a tongue that he knew well, but had
never heard. Her tones filled him with an ecstasy near to
pain. He sat beside her on the faery bank, and she told
him many things: divine, stupendous, perilous things;
dire as the secret of life; sweet as the lore of oblivion;
strange and immemorable as the lost knowledge of sleep.
But she did not tell him her name, nor the secret of her

essence; and still he knew not if she were ghost or woman, goddess or spirit.

Something there was in her speech of time and its mystery; something of that which lies forever beyond time; something of the grey shadow of doom that waits upon world and sun; something of love, that pursues an elusive, perishing fire; of death, the soil from which all flowers spring; of life, that is a mirage on the frozen void.

For a while Tortha was content merely to listen. A high rapture filled him, he felt the awe of a mortal in the presence of a deity. Then, as he grew accustomed to his situation, the womanlike beauty of the Sybil spoke to him no less eloquently than her words. Vacillant, by degrees, like a tide that lifts to some unearthly moon, there rose up in his heart the human love that was half of his adoration. He felt a delirium of desire, mixed with the vertigo of one who has climbed to an impossible height. He saw only the white loveliness of her divinity; and no longer did he hear clearly the high wisdom of her speech.

The Sybil paused in her ineffable discourse; and somehow, with slow, stumbling words, he dared to tell her of his love.

She made no answer, gave no gesture of assent or denial. But when he had done, she regarded him strangely; whether with love or pity, sadness or joy, he could not tell. Then, swiftly, she bent forward and kissed his brow with her pallid lips. Their kiss was like the searing of fire or ice. But, mad with his supreme longing, Tortha strove rashly to embrace the Sybil.

Dreadfully, unutterably, she seemed to change in his arms as he clasped her — to become a frozen corpse that had lain for ages in a floe-built tomb — a leper-white mummy in whose frosted eyes he read the horror of the ultimate void. Then she was a thing that had no form or name — a dark corruption that flowed and eddied in his arms — a hueless dust, a flight of gleaming atoms, that rose between his evaded fingers. Then there was nothing — and the faery-tinted flowers about him were changing also, were crumbling swiftly, were falling beneath flurries of white snow. The vast and violet heaven, the tall slim trees, the magic, unreflecting stream — the very ground under him — all had vanished amid the universal, whirling flakes.

It seemed to Tortha that he was plunging dizzily into some deep gulf together with that chaos of driven snows. Gradually, as he fell, the air grew clear about him, and he appeared to hang suspended above the receding, dissolving storm. He was alone in a still, funereal, starless heaven; and below, at an awesome and giddying distance, he saw the dimly glittering reaches of a land sheathed with glacial ice from horizon to far-curved horizon. The snows had vanished from the dead air; and a searing cold, like the breath of the infinite ether, was about Tortha.

All this he saw and felt for a timeless instant. Then, with the swiftness of a meteor, he resumed his fall toward the frozen continent. And like the rushing flame of a meteor, his consciousness dimmed and went out on the bleak air even as he fell.

Tortha had been seen by the half-savage people of the mountains as he disappeared in the sudden storm that had come mysteriously from Polarion. Later, when the blinding flurries had died down, they found him lying on the glacier. They tended him with rough care and uncouth skill, marvelling much at the white mark that had been imprinted like a fiery brand on his sunswart brow. The flesh was seared deeply; and the mark was shaped like the pressure of lips. But they could not know that the never-fading mark had been left by the kiss of the White Sybil.

Slowly, Tortha won back to some measure of his former strength. But ever afterward there was a cloudy dimness in his mind, a blur of unresolving shadow, like the dazzlement in eyes that have looked on some insupportable light.

Among those who tended him was a pale maiden, not uncomely; and Tortha took her for the Sybil in the darkness that had come upon him. The maiden's name was Illara, and Tortha loved her in his delusion; and, forgetful of his kin and his friends in Cerngoth, he dwelt with the mountain people thereafter, taking Illara to wife and making the songs of the little tribe. For the most part, he was happy in his belief that the Sybil had returned to him; and Illara, in her way, was content, being not the first of mortal women whose lover had remained faithful to a divine illusion.

CHINOISERIE

Ling Yang, the poet, sits all day in his willow-hidden hut by the river side, and dreams of the Lady Moy. Spring and the swallows have returned from the timeless isles of amaranth, further than the flight of sails in the unknown south; the silver buds of the willow are breaking into gold; and delicate jade-green reeds have begun to push their way among the brown and yellow rushes of yesteryear. But Ling Yang is heedless of the brightening azure, the light that lengthens; and he has no eye for the northward flight of the waterfowl, and the passing of the last clouds, that melt and vanish in the flames of an amber sunset. For him, there is no season save that moon of waning summer in which he first met the Lady Moy. But a sorrow deeper than the sorrow of autumn abides in his heart: for the heart of Moy is colder to him than high mountain snows above a tropic valley; and all the songs he has made for her, the songs of the flute and the songs of the lute, have found no favor in her hearing.

Leagues away, in her pavilion of scarlet lacquer and ebony, the Lady Moy reclines on a couch piled with sapphire-coloured silks. All day, through the gathering gold of the willow-foliage, she watches the placid lake, on whose surface the pale-green lily pads have begun to widen. Beside her, in a turquoise-studded binding, there lie the verses of the poet Ling Yung, who lived six centuries ago, and who sang in all his songs the praise of the Lady Loy, who disdained him. Moy has no need to peruse them any longer, for they live in her memory even as upon the written page. And, sighing, she dreams ever of the great poet, Ling Yung, and of the melancholy romance that inspired his songs, and wonders enviously at the odd disdain that was shown toward him by the Lady Loy.

19

THE RAJA AND THE TIGER

There was more than one reason why Bently did not view his appointment as British Resident at Shaitanabad with enthusiasm. The climate was reported to be particularly hot even for India, the population largely composed of snakes, tigers, and wild boars, and the attitude of the natives from the Raja down unfriendly. The last Resident had died of sunstroke, so it was said, and the one before him departed suddenly for an unknown destination without taking the trouble to apply for leave of absence. But as somebody had to occupy the position, Bently went to Shaitanabad; from the nearest railway station one hundred miles by camel and bullock cart over parched hills and sandy desert.

His early impressions of the place were hardly reassuring. His first glimpse of it was from the summit of a cactus-covered hill through a red haze of dust-laden heat. The principal feature which caught his eye was the Raja's fortress-palace perched on a high rock on the northeast side and grimly overlooking the flat-roofed city. It was known as the Nahargarh, or Tiger Fort. For the rest Shaitanabad may be summed up as a place of narrow, irregular alleys, bazaars with shops little larger than dry-goods boxes, bad smells, a perpetual plague of insects, gaily clothed people, and a general Arabian Nights atmosphere. A thousand years ago it was the same, and so it will be a thousand years hence. The local temperature was a 120° in the shade, sometimes more. Except the Resident, there were no other Englishmen in the place, not even a missionary. That is sufficient testimony as to Shaitanabad's character.

Bently regarded it as fortunate that the Residency was situated outside the city, and that his predecessor's staff of Bengali and Rajput servants were waiting to receive him. A bath, a fairly well-cooked meal, and a good night's rest, in spite of the heat, removed the exhaustion of the journey and made the outlook appear more satisfactory.

His first duty being to call on the Raja, he early proceeded to the palace accompanied by his servant, Lal Das. Ascending a flight of steps cut in the towering sandstone rock, which was the only means of access to the fort, Bently passed through a great gate into a courtyard. There he was left to stand in the full rays of the Indian sun while the Raja's attendants went in to announce the Resident's arrival. Finally they returned and conducted him through a deep veranda into a hall, from which another room opened. This room, carpeted with Persian rugs and hung with rare kinkhab draperies, seemed cool and pleasant after the heat without.

The Raja, Chumbu Singh, was seated on a cushioned *gadi*, surrounded by several attendants. He was a tall, slender man of about forty, and wore the peculiar Rajput side whiskers. His attire consisted of a pearl-embroidered coat, trousers of white tussah silk, and an elaborately embroidered turban. One hand toyed with the gem-encrusted hilt of a short sword stuck in a broad silk cummerbund.

At this first meeting conversation was short and formal. The Raja asked after Bently's health, and requested his opinion of such matters as the climate. He spoke fluent English, and seemed well educated and intelligent.

"I hope you will like Shaitanabad," he said, finally. "Sport here is good. If at any time you care to hunt tigers, I shall be glad to place all the facilities in my power at your disposal."

Bently retired on the whole rather favorably impressed with the Raja and inclined to treat certain adverse reports of his conduct as exaggerated. Native princes are always more or less prone to irritation at the ways of British Residents. Probably such was the basis of Chumbu Singh's offense in British official quarters.

During the next two or three weeks Bently thought he had reason to be pleased at his judgment of native character. Chumbu Singh fell so readily into certain administrative reforms proposed by Bently that there appeared little doubt of his earnestness to walk in the path of modern progress. So far things looked much better than he had been led to anticipate, even the temperature dropping to 98° at midnight. It was after the settlement of a land ownership case, in which Bently's assistance had been requested, that the Raja made a proposal.

"I have arranged for a tiger hunt tonight," he said. "Would you like to go?"

Bently eagerly responded in the affirmative.

"This is a terrible animal, Sahib," continued the Raja. "He has killed many people. His den is in the hills — an old cave temple, haunted, my people say, by ghosts and devils. However that may be, the tiger is many devils in himself. He stalks both cattle and villagers in broad day light, and kills not only when hungry, but out of the devilishness of his heart. We have planned to get him at the cave."

When the last rays of the sun had faded from the hot red sandstone of the Nahargarh, and the gray veil of dusk had fallen over Shaitanabad, Chumbu Singh and several followers came to the Residency to announce that all was ready. They were armed and mounted on wiry Baluchi ponies. Bently joined them, accompanied by Lal Das, and the party set off across the rapidly darkening plain. Their destination, as indicated by Chumbu Singh, was a mass of low-lying, jungle-clad hills two miles to the northeast. The plain, or rather desert, between was barren with scarce a tree or shrub, and its monotony was broken only by a series of nasty nullahs or gulleys, which gave much trouble, necessitating careful horsemanship and slow traveling.

Reaching the hills without mishaps, the horses were left near an old tomb in charge of the servants. The Raja, Bently, Lal Das, and two Rajputs continued afoot. They first followed a bullock trail, and then a narrow foot-path, one of the Rajputs acting as guide. The path, winding up and down, through cactus jungle, deep ravines, and among great boulders, led well into the hills.

The moon had risen, and as they emerged from a patch of jungle, Bently saw the cave temple of which Chumbu Singh had spoken. It was in a steep hillside, where the formation changed from sandstone to light granite. In front was a level space overgrown with cactus, jungle plants, and a few larger trees. There were three entrances, the central one being about fifteen feet high, and the other two smaller. The larger one was open, but the others were choked with debris.

The hunters toiled up the hillside, scrambling over boulders and through the thick scrub. There was no path, and it was not pleasant travelling. A handful of cactus spines, even on a moonlit night in the presence of ancient and interesting ruins, is more productive of profanity than enthusiasm.

"This is the ancient temple of Jains," said the Raja when they at last came panting to the entrance.

Bently peered within to behold the moonlight shining on huge indistinct figures, old forgotten gods carved in the solid granite. There were also great footprints in the thick dust, evidently those of the tiger. Undoubtedly he was a monster animal, for Bently had never seen pads to equal them.

The two Rajputs examined the pads carefully, and gave it as their opinion that the tiger had crept forth, bent on stalking about nightfall, and would probably not return until morning. They were sure he was not in the cave. The Raja seemed annoyed at the prospect of a long wait, and abused the Rajputs for not arranging matters so that they might have arrived at the cave earlier and so intercepted the tiger.

"I owe you many apologies," he said, turning Bently. "You see what comes of trusting to these fellows. But since it is such an effort to get here, I suggest that we wait for the tiger."

"Certainly," agreed Bently. "I am willing to wait as long as you like for a shot at that beast."

"Very well," the Raja nodded. "In the meantime suppose we take a look at the cave temple. It is an interesting place, of its kind without equal in India."

To this Bently readily assented. Thereupon the Raja sent off one of the Rajputs and Lal Das with an order for the rest of the retainers to keep watch in case the tiger returned unexpectedly. The other Rajput then produced a torch, and the party of three entered the cave. First they passed through a sort of peristyle, or antechamber, which, thirty yards from the entrance, opened into a vast grotto. This was the main excavation. Huge stone pillars, elaborately sculptured, supported the roof, and around the sides great gods and goddesses of the Jain mythology, called Arhats, glared downward. The torch illuminated dimly, leaving much in shadow, and in the shadow imagination created strange fantasies. A narrow passage from the grotto ended in a smaller chamber littered with fallen fragments. It was more than once necessary to climb over some god whose face was in the dust. Another short passage led to an arched entrance two-thirds blocked with debris.

"We cannot go any further," said the Raja, "but if you take the torch and climb up on that pile, you will be able to see into a greater cave beyond. My superstitious retainers believe that it is the abode of ghosts and devils, the guardians of the temple."

Bently's curiosity was stimulated. Torch in hand he surmounted the obstruction, and peered into a gulf of black darkness. He seemed on the verge of a great precipice, the limits and bottom of which the torchlight failed to reach. From far beneath he fancied he caught a splash of water tumbling over a rocky bed, and strange echoes floated upward, but he could see nothing. It was an appalling abyss, which, for all he knew, might sink into the foundations of the earth.

Suddenly he received a violent push from behind, accompanied by a muttered curse hurled from the Raja's lips. Bently tumbled forward, and, in doing so, threw out an arm wildly to save himself. It caught the barrel of the Raja's rifle, swept it from his grasp, and hurled it clattering into the chasm beneath. Bently promptly followed the Raja's rifle down a steep crumbling slope to what would have been certain death had his own rifle not brought him up with a jerk by becoming lodged to half its length between two rocks. As it were, there he hung in midair with the buttress of his rifle for his only support. A shower of following pebbles swept on down into nothingness.

For some moments he remained almost stunned by the peril of the situation, but presently his mind began to gather in the slender chances of escape. He had apparently been brought up with his back against a side-wall of rock and with one foot resting on a narrow projection. Reaching out a hand, and groping with it, he discovered that the narrow projection was one of a flight of irregular steps cut in the rock and leading upward. If a hazardous foothold, he presumed it had been used at some period, and decided to tempt its course.

He balanced himself carefully, and disengaging his rifle, crept slowly upward step by step. Once his foot slipped, and he almost fell, but throwing himself inward he found he had stumbled into the entrance of a narrow passage. That meant safety from the chasm at any rate, and he gave vent to a huge breath of relief. His next act was to test the springs of his rifle, and so far as he was able to judge in the darkness he was further gratified to find that it was uninjured. Then he went cautiously forward, guiding his progress by a hand on the side-wall. Presently he came to a broad flight of steps partly choked up with fallen debris. Climbing up this, he emerged into the grotto of the temple.

Then he drew back suddenly. A coughing snarl echoed through the cavern. Bently softly moved behind the stone image of a god, and looked out from its shadow. From a cleft in the roof of the temple a stream of moonlight fell within, and toned with silver the yellow body and velvet stripes of a monster tiger. It also shone upon the prostrate forms of the Raja and his Rajput retainer, held beneath the huge paws of the Lord of the Jungle. Again the coughing snarl echoed through the temple. The eyes of the beast flashed with savage thirst for blood as it lowered its head to plunge its fangs into the throat of one of its victims.

Bently raised his rifle to the shoulder, took steady aim, and fired. A terrific roar shook the stone gods, a gigantic convulsion seized upon the body of the tiger as it rolled over. Bently fired again, and then strode from his place of concealment. Another shot at closer range finished the death struggle of the tiger. Its last breath went forth in a choking growl of defiance.

It took but a cursory examination to convince Bently

that both the Raja and the Rajput were past rendering any account of their treachery on this earth, and a lack of response to his shouts made it plain that the Raja's retainers had promptly bolted when the tiger unexpectedly returned. The Raja and the Rajput has thus been left to encounter the powerful beast unarmed.

How Bently regained the Residency was a matter he was unable to explain except by instinct, but daylight had already broken when he reached the compound. Then he acted with swift decision.

He sent orders for the Raja's retainers to appear at the Residency for an investigation, which eventually led to a thorough exploration of the temple. By another entrance the bottom of the abyss was gained, and sundry relics discovered there proved how the Raja had relieved himself of the undesirable presence of those who had interfered with his dubious proceedings.

THE JUSTICE
OF THE ELEPHANT

Nikhal *Singh*, Rajah of Anapur, was acquiring the obese complacency of middle age; and his memories were blurred and befogged by a liberal use of Rajput opium. It was seldom that he recalled Ameera; though, as a general rule, an unfaithful woman is not the easiest thing in the world to forget. But Nikhal Singh had possessed so many wives and concubines; and one more or less was of no great importance, even though she had been eyed like the sloe and footed like the gazelle and had preferred an elephant-driver to a Rajah. And as Nikhal Singh grew older, and became wearier of women and fonder of opium, such matters were even less memorable or worthy of consideration.

However, the incident had angered him greatly at the time; and the doom he devised for Ameera was the most atrocious one conceivable. Her story was long remembered and whispered in the royal zenana; though whether or not the example had served to deter others from similar derelictions is a moot problem.

Ameera was a dancing-girl, and therefore of low birth; and her rise in the Rajah's favor had not been regarded with unqualified approval by his legitimate wives. Under the circumstances, it was highly unwise for Ameera to carry on a love affair with the comely young elephant-driver, Rama Das; for there were many jealous eyes to note the amour, and jealous tongues to bear tattle thereof to Nikhal Singh. Ameera had been watched; and a man was seen leaving her apartments in the early morning hours. The man was not positively identified as Rama Das; but the presence of anyone save the Rajah in those sacrosanct purlieus was enough to damn the unfortunate girl.

The punishment inflicted by Nikhal Singh was no less swift than dreadful. The girl was condemned to a death usually reserved for the lowest criminals; and her suspected lover, Rama Das, by a refinement of Rajput cruelty, was chosen to her executioner. She was made to kneel and place her head on a block of stone in the palace courtyard; and thereupon the great elephant ridden by Rama Das, at a signal from the driver, lifted one of his enormous hoofs and brought it down on the head of the dancing-girl, crushing her to an instant pulp. During the awful ordeal, no sign of recognition or emotion was betrayed either by Rama Das or Ameera; and the gloating Rajah was perhaps disappointed in this respect. A day or two afterward the young elephant-driver disappeared from Anapur; and no one knew whether he had been secretly made away with by Nikhal Singh or had vanished of his own accord.

Ten years had now passed; and the affair was overlaid, even in the minds of the Rajah's eldest wives, by a score of later scandals and by the petty happenings of the palace. And when the position of mahout to Ragna, the huge elephant that bore the Rajah himself on all formal occasions, became vacant through death, no one would have connected the half-forgotten Rama Das with the new applicant, Ram Chandar, who vowed his fitness to take charge of Ragna and offered credentials testifying to years of faithful and efficient service to the Maharajah of a state in Bundelcund. And least of all would it have occurred to Nikhal Singh himself that the grave, taciturn, heavy-bearded Ram Chandar and the blithe, beardless Rama Das were the same person.

Somehow, though there were many other applicants, Ram Chandar insinuated himself into the desired position. And since he was a competent driver, who had obviously mastered the language of elephants down to its last and most subtle inflection, no one, not even his fellow mahouts, found reason to disapprove or criticize his appointment. Ragna also appeared to like his new driver; and that ideal confidence and understanding which often exists between the mahout and the animal soon sprang up between these two. Ragna, after the fashion of a well-tutored elephant, was wise and erudite in regard to all that it was proper for him to know; but he learned some new manners and graces beneath the instruction of Ram Chandar; and was even taught in private one or two tricks that are not usually part of the curriculum of a state elephant. Of these latter, no one dreamt; and Ram Chandar preserved an inscrutable silence. And Nikhal Singh was wholly unaware of the strange, sardonic, sinister regard with which he was watched by the new mahout from Bundelcund.

Nikhal Singh had grown fonder than ever of his opium, and cared less and less for other pleasures or distractions. But now, in his fortieth rear, for political reasons, it was agreed upon by his ministers that he must take another wife. The Ranee had recently died without leaving him a male heir; and the young daughter of the neighboring Rajah of Ayalmere was selected as her successor. All the necessary arrangements and elaborate protocols were made; and the day was set for the marriage. Nikhal Singh was secretly bored by the prospect but was publicly resigned to his royal duty. The feelings of the bride, perhaps, were even more problematical.

The day of the marriage dawned in torrid saffron. A great procession coming from Ayalmere was to bring the bride into Anapur; and Nikhal Singh, with another stately procession, was to meet her outside the gates of his capital.

It was a gorgeous ceremony. Nikhal Singh, seated in

a golden and jewel-crusted howdah on the superb elephant Ragna, passed through the streets of Anapur followed by the court dignitaries on other elephants and a
small army of horsemen, all splendidly caparisoned.
There was much firing of jezails and cannon by the soldiers and banging of musical instruments among the
populace. The mahout, Ram Chandar, grave and impassive as usual, sat on Ragna's neck. Nikhal Singh, who had
fortified himself with a large lump of his favorite drug,
was equally impassive on his broidered cushions in the
howdah.

The procession emerged through the open gate of
Anapur, and beheld at some distance, in a cloud of
summer dust, the approach of the bride and her attendants, forming an array no less magnificent and sump-
tuous than that which was headed by Nikhal Singh.

As the two processions neared each other, an event
occurred which was not a pre-arranged part of the ceremonial. At a secret signal from Ram Chandar, perceived
and understood only by the elephant himself, Ragna
suddenly halted, reached into the great howdah with his
trunk, seized Nikhal Singh in a tenacious embrace, and
haling the Rajah forth in a most undignified and igno-
minious manner, deposited him on his the knees in the
road and forced him to bow his head in the dust before
bride's approaching litter. Then, almost before his action
was comprehended by the stupefied throng, Ragna
raised one of his front hoofs and calmly proceeded to
crush the Rajah's head into a flat, formless jelly. Then,
trumpeting wildly, menacing all who stood in his way,
and apparently defying the frantic signals and commands of his driver, Ragna plunged through the crowd
and quickly vanished in the nearby jungle, still carrying
Ram Chandar and the empty howdah.

Amid the confusion and consternation that prevailed, it was assumed that Ragna had been seized by the vicious madness to which elephants are sometimes liable. When a semblance of order had been restored, he was followed by a troop of the Rajah's horsemen, armed with jezails. They found him an hour later, browsing peacefully in a jungle-glade without his driver, and dispatched him with a volley, not trusting his appearance of renewed mildness.

The assumption that Ragna had gone *musth* was universal; and no one thought of Rama Das and the death of Ameera, ten years before. However, the disappearance of the new mahout, Ram Chandar, was no less a mystery than the earlier vanishment of Rama Das, if anyone had remembered to draw the parallel. The body of Ram Chandar was never found, and no one knew to a certainty whether he had been killed by Ragna in the thick jungle or had run away from Anapur through fear of being held responsible for Ragna's behavior. But mad - elephants are prone to wreak their malignity on all accessible victims, even their own mahouts; so it was considered very unlikely that Ram Chandar could have escaped.

THE KISS OF ZORAIDA

With one backward look at the bowery suburbs of Damascus, and the street that was peopled only by the long, faint shadows of a crescent moon, Selim dropped from the high wall among the leafing almonds and flowering lilacs of Abdur Ali's garden. The night was almost sultry, and the air was steeped with a distilled languor of voluptuous perfume. Even if he had been in some other garden, in another city, Selim could not have breathed that perfume without thinking of Zoraida, the young wife of Abdur Ali. Evening after evening, for the past fortnight, during her lord and master's absence, she had met him among the lilacs, till he had grown to associate the very odor of her hair and the savor of her lips with their fragrance.

The garden was silent, except for a silver-lisping fountain; and no leaf or petal stirred in the balmy stillness. Abdur Ali had gone to Aleppo on urgent business and was not expected back for several more days; so the slightly tepid thrill of anticipation which Selim felt was untinged by any thought of danger. The whole affair, even from the beginning, had been as safe as that sort of thing could possibly be: Zoraida was Abdur Ali's wife, so there were no jealous women who might tattle to their common lord; and the servants and eunuchs of the household, like Zoraida herself, hated the severe and elderly jewel-merchant. It had been unnecessary even to bribe them into complaisance. Everything and everyone had helped to facilitate the amour. In fact, it was all too easy; and Selim was beginning to weary a little of this heavy-scented garden and the oversweet affection of Zoraida. Perhaps he would not come again after tonight, or tomorrow night. . . . There were other women, no less fair than the jeweler's wife, whom he had not kissed so often . . . or had not kissed at all.

He stepped forward among the flower-burdened bushes. Was there a figure standing in the shadow, near the fountain? The figure was dim, and darkly muffled, but it must be Zoraida. She had never failed to meet him there, she was ever the first at their rendezvous. Sometimes she had taken him into the luxurious harem; and sometimes, on warm evenings like this, they had spent their long hours of passion beneath the stars, amid the lilacs and almonds.

As Selim approached, he wondered why she did not rush to meet him, as was her wont. Perhaps she had not yet seen him. He called softly: "Zoraida!"

The waiting figure emerged from the shadow. It was not Zoraida, but Abdur Ali. The faint moon-rays glinted on the dull iron barrel and bright silver frettings of a heavy pistol which the old merchant held in his hand.

"You wish to see Zoraida?" The tone was harsh, metallically bitter.

Selim, to say the least, was taken aback. It was all too plain that his affair with Zoraida had been discovered, and that Abdur Ali had returned from Aleppo before the appointed time to catch him in a trap. The predicament was more than disagreeable, for a young man who had thought to spend the evening with a much-enamoured mistress. And Abdur Ali's direct query was disconcerting. Selim was unable to think of an apt or judicious answer.

"Come, thou shalt see her." Selim felt the jealous fury, but not the savage irony, that underlay the words. He was full of unpleasant premonitions, most of which concerned himself rather than Zoraida. He knew that he could not look for mercy from this austere and terrible old man; and the probabilities before him were such as to preclude more than a passing thought of what might

have befallen, or would befall, Zoraida. Selim was something of an egoist; and he could hardly have claimed
(except for the ear of Zoraida) that he was deeply in love.
His self-solicitude, under the circumstances, was perhaps to be expected, even if not wholly to be admired.

Abdur Ali had covered Selim with the pistol. The
young man realized uncomfortably that he himself was
unarmed, except for his yataghan. Even as he was remembering this, two more figures came forward from
amid the lilac-shadows. They were the eunuchs, Cassim
and Mustafa, who guarded Abdur Ali's harem, and
whom the lovers believed friendly to their intrigue. Each
of the giant blacks was armed with a drawn scimitar.
Mustafa stationed himself at Selim's right hand and
Cassim at his left. He could see the whites of their eyes as
they watched him with impassable vigilance.

"Now," said Abdur Ali, "you are about to enjoy the
singular privilege of being admitted to my harem. This
privilege, I believe, you have arrogated to yourself on
certain former occasions, and without my knowledge.
Tonight I shall grant it myself; though I doubt if there are
many who would follow my example. Come: Zoraida is
waiting for you, and you must not disappoint her, nor
delay any longer. You are later than usual at the rendezvous, as I happen to know."

With the blacks beside him, with Abdur Ali and the
levelled pistol in his rear, Selim traversed the dim garden
and entered the courtyard of the jewel-merchant's house.
It was like a journey in some evil dream; and nothing
appeared wholly real to the young man. Even when he
stood in the harem interior, by the soft light of Saracenic
lamps of wrought brass, and saw the familiar divans
with their deep-hued cushions and coverings, the rare
Turkoman and Persian rugs, the taborets of Indian ebony
freaked with precious metals and mother-of-pearl, he

could not dispel his feeling of strange dubiety.

In his terror and bewilderment, amid the rich furnishings and somber splendor, he did not see Zoraida for a moment. Abdur Ali perceived his confusion and pointed to one of the couches.

"Hast thou no greeting for Zoraida?" The low tone was indescribably sardonic and ferocious.

Zoraida, wearing the scanty harem costume of bright silks in which she was wont to receive her lover, was lying on the sullen crimson fabrics of the divan. She was very still, and seemed to be asleep. Her face was whiter than usual, though she had always been a little pale; and the soft, childlike features, with their hint of luxurious roundness, wore a vaguely troubled expression, with a touch of bitterness about the mouth. Selim approached her, but she did not stir.

"Speak to her," snarled the old man. His eyes burned like two spots of slowly eating fire in the brown and crumpled parchment of his face.

Selim was unable to utter a word. He had begun to surmise the truth; and the situation overwhelmed him with a horrible despair.

"What? thou hast no greeting for one who loved thee so dearly?" The words were like the dripping of some corrosive acid.

"What hast thou done to her?" said Selim after a while. He could not look at Zoraida any longer; nor could he lift his eyes to meet those of Abdur Ali.

"I have dealt with her very gently. As thou seest, I have not marred in any way the perfection of her beauty — there is no wound, and not even the mark of a blow, on her white body. Was I not more generous . . . to leave her thus . . . for thee?"

Selim was not a coward, as men go; yet he gave an involuntary shudder.

"But . . . thou hast not told me."

"It was a rare and precious poison, which slays immediately and with little pain. A drop of it would have been enough — or even so much as still remains upon her lips. She drank it of her own choice. I was merciful to her — as I shall be to thee."

"I am at thy disposal," said Selim with all the hardihood he could muster.

The jewel-dealer's face became a mask of malignity, like that of some avenging fiend.

"My eunuchs know their master, and they will slice thee limb from limb and member from member if I give the word."

Selim looked at the two negroes. They returned his gaze with impassive eyes that were utterly devoid of all interest, either friendly or unfriendly. The light ran without a quiver along their gleaming muscles and upon their glittering swords.

"What is thy will? Dost thou mean to kill me?"

"I have no intention of slaying thee myself. Thy death will come from another source."

Selim looked again at the armed eunuchs.

"No, it will not be that — unless you prefer it."

"In Allah's name, what doest thou mean, then?" The tawny brown of Selim's face had turned ashen with horror of suspense.

"Thy death will be one which any true lover would envy," said Abdur Ali.

Selim was powerless to ask another question. His nerves were beginning to crumble under the ordeal. The dead woman on the couch, the malevolent old man with his baleful half-hints and his obvious implacability, the muscular negroes who would hew a man into collops at their master's word — all were enough to break down the courage of hardier men than he.

He became aware that Abdur Ali was speaking once more.

"I have brought thee to thy mistress. But it would seem that thou art not a very ardent lover."

"In the name of the Prophet, cease thy mockery."

Abdur Ali did not seem to hear the tortured cry.

"It is true, of course, that she could not reply even if thou shouldst speak to her. But her lips are as fair as ever, even if they are growing a little cold with thy unloverlike delay. Hast thou no kiss to lay upon them, in memory of all the other kisses they have taken — and given?"

Selim was again speechless. Finally:

"But you said there was a poison which —"

"Yes, and I told thee the truth. Even the touch of thy lips to hers, where a trace of the poison lingers, will be enough to cause thy death." There was an awful gloating in Abdur Ali's voice.

Selim shivered and looked again at Zoraida. Aside from her utter stillness and pallor, and the faintly bitter expression about the mouth, she differed in no apparent wise from the woman who had lain so often in his arms. Yet the very knowledge that she was dead was enough to make her seem unspeakably strange and even repulsive to Selim. It was hard to associate this still, marmoreal being with the affectionate mistress who had always welcomed him with eager smiles and caresses.

"Is there no other way?" Selim's question was little louder than a whisper.

"There is none. And you delay too long." Abdur Ali made a sign to the negroes, who stepped closer to Selim, lifting their swords in the lamplight.

"Unless thou dost my bidding, thy hands will be sliced off at the wrists," the jeweler went on. "The next blows will sever a small portion of each forearm. Then a brief attention will be given to other parts, before returning to the arms. I am sure thou wilt prefer the other death."

Selim stooped above the couch where Zoraida lay. Terror — the abject terror of death — was his one emotion. He had wholly forgotten his love for Zoraida, had forgotten her kisses and endearments. He feared the strange, pale woman before him as much as he had once desired her.

"Make haste." The voice of Abdur Ali was steely as the lifted scimitars.

Selim bent over and kissed Zoraida on the mouth. Her lips were not entirely cold, but there was a queer, bitter taste. Of course, it must the poison. The thought was hardly formulated when a searing agony seemed to run through all his veins. He could no longer see Zoraida, in the blinding flames that appeared before him and filled the room like ever-widening suns; and he did not know that he had fallen forward on the couch across her body. Then the flames began to shrink with great swiftness and went out in a swirl of soft gloom. Selim felt that he was sinking into a great gulf, and that someone (whose name he could not remember) was sinking beside him. Then, all at once, he was alone, and was losing even the sense of solitude . . . till there was nothing but darkness and oblivion.

THE GHOUL

During the reign of the Caliph Vathek, a young man of good repute and family, named Noureddin Hassan, was haled before the Cadi Ahmed ben Becar at Bussorah. Now Noureddin was a comely youth, of open mind and gentle mien; and great was the astonishment of the Cadi and of all others present when they heard the charges that were preferred against him. He was accused of having slain seven people one by one, on seven successive nights, and of having left the corpses in a cemetery near Bussorah, where they were found lying with their bodies and members devoured in a fearsome manner, as if by jackals. Of the people he was said to have slain, three were women, two were traveling merchants, one was a mendicant, and one a gravedigger.

Ahmed ben Becar was filled with the learning and wisdom of honorable years, and withal was possessed of much perspicacity. But he was deeply perplexed by the strangeness and atrocity of these crimes and by the mild demeanor and well-bred aspect of Noureddin Hassan, which he could in no wise reconcile with them. He heard in silence the testimony of witnesses who had seen Noureddin bearing on his shoulders the body of a woman at yester-eve in the cemetery; and others who on several occasions had observed him coming from the neighborhood at unseemly hours when only thieves and murderers would be abroad. Then, having considered all these, he questioned the youth closely.

"Noureddin Hassan," he said, "thou hast been charged with crimes of exceeding foulness, which thy bearing and lineaments belie. Is there haply some explanation of these things by which thou canst clear thyself, or in some measure mitigate the heinousness of thy deeds, if so it be that thou art guilty? I adjure thee to tell me the truth in this matter."

Now Noureddin Hassan arose before the Cadi; and the heaviness of extreme shame and sorrow was visible on his countenance.

"Alas, O Cadi," he replied, "for the charges that have been brought against me are indeed true. It was I and no other, who slew these people; nor can I offer an extenuation of my act."

The Cadi was sorely grieved and astonished when he heard this answer.

"I must perforce believe thee," he said sternly. "But thou hast confessed a thing which will make thy name henceforward an abomination in the ears and mouths of men. I command thee to tell me why these crimes were committed, and what offense these persons had given thee, or what injury they had done to thee; or if perchance thou slewest them for gain, like a common robber."

"There was neither offense given nor injury wrought by any of them against me," replied Noureddin. "And I did not kill them for their money or belongings or apparel, since I had no need of such things, and, aside from that, have always been an honest man."

"Then," cried Ahmed ben Becar, greatly puzzled, "what was thy reason if it was none of these?"

Now the face of Noureddin Hassan grew heavier still with sorrow; and he bowed his head in a shamefaced manner that bespoke the utterness of profound remorse. And standing thus before the Cadi, he told this story:

The reversals of fortune, O Cadi, are swift and grievous, and beyond the foreknowing or advertence of man. Alas! for less than a fortnight agone I was the happiest and most guiltless of mortals, with no thought of wrongdoing toward anyone. I was wedded to Amina, the daughter of the jewel-merchant Aboul Cogia; and I loved her deeply and was much beloved by her in turn; and moreover we were at this time anticipating the birth of our first child. I had inherited from my father a rich estate and many slaves; the cares of life were light upon my shoulders; and I had, it would seem, every reason to count myself among those Allah had blest with an earthly foretaste of Heaven.

Judge, then, the excessive nature of my grief when Amina died in the same hour when she was to have been delivered. From that time, in the dire extremity of my lamentation, I was as one bereft of light and knowledge; I was deaf to all those who sought to condole with me, and blind to their friendly offices.

After the burial of Amina my sorrow became a veritable madness, and I wandered by night to her grave in the cemetery near Bussorah and flung myself prostrate before the newly lettered tombstone, on the earth that had been digged that very day. My senses deserted me, and I knew not how long I remained on the damp clay beneath the cypresses, while the horn of a decrescent moon arose in the heavens.

Then, in my stupor of abandonment, I heard a terrible voice that bade me rise from the ground on which I was lying. And lifting my head a little, I saw a hideous demon of gigantic frame and stature, with eyes of scarlet fire beneath brows that were coarse as tangled rootlets, and fangs that overhung a cavernous mouth, and earth-black teeth longer and sharper than those of the hyena. And the demon said to me:

"I am a ghoul, and it is my office to devour the bodies of the dead. I have now come to claim the corpse that was interred today beneath the soil on which thou art lying in a fashion so unmannerly. Begone, for I have fasted since yester-night, and I am much anhungered."

Now, at the sight of this demon, and the sound of

his dreadful voice, and the still more dreadful meaning of his words, I was like to have swooned with terror on the cold clay. But I recovered myself in a manner, and besought him, saying:

"Spare this grave, I implore thee; for she who lies buried therein is dearer to me than any living mortal; and I would not that her fair body should be the provender of an unclean demon such as thou."

At this the ghoul was angered, and I thought that he would have done me some bodily violence. But again I besought him, swearing by Allah and Mohammed with many solemn oaths that I would grant him anything procurable and would do for him any favor that lay in the power of man if he would leave undespoiled the new-made grave of Amina. And the ghoul was somewhat mollified, and he said:

"If thou wilt indeed perform for me a certain service, I shall do as thou askest." And I replied:

"There is no service, whatsoever its nature, that I will not do for thee in this connection, and I pray thee to name thy desire."

Then the ghoul said: "It is this, that thou shalt bring me each night, for eight successive nights, the body of one whom thou hast slain with thine own hand. Do this, and I shall neither devour nor dig the body that lies interred hereunder."

Now was I seized by utter horror and despair, since I had bound myself in all honor to grant the ghoul his hideous requirement. And I begged him to change the terms of the stipulation, saying to him:

"Is it needful to thee, O eater of corpses, that the bodies should be those of people whom I myself have slain?"

And the ghoul said: "Yea, for all others would be the natural provender of myself or of my kin in any event. I adjure thee by the promise thou hast given to meet me here tomorrow night, when darkness has wholly fallen or as soon thereafter as thou art able, bringing the first of the eight bodies."

So saying, he strode off among the cypresses, and began to dig in another newly made grave at a little distance from that of Amina.

I left the graveyard in even direr anguish than when I had come, thinking of that which I must do in fulfillment of my sworn promise, to preserve the body of Amina from the demon. I know not how I survived the ensuing day, torn as I was between sorrow for the dead and my horror of the coming night with its repugnant duty.

When darkness had descended I went forth by stealth to a lonely road near the cemetery; and waiting there amid the low-grown branches of the trees, I slew the first passer with a sword and carried his body to the spot appointed by the ghoul. And each night thereafter, for six more nights, I returned to the same vicinity and repeated this deed, slaying always the very first who came, whether man or woman, or merchant or beggar or gravedigger. And the ghoul awaited me on each occasion, and would begin to devour his provender in my presence, with small thanks and scant ceremony. Seven persons did I slay in all, till only one was wanting to complete the agreed number; and the person I slew yester-night was a woman, even as the witnesses have testified. All this I did with utmost repugnance and regret, and sustained only by the remembrance of my plighted word and the fate which would befall the corpse of Amina if I should break the bond.

This, O Cadi, is all my story. Alas! For these lamentable crimes have availed me not, and I have failed in wholly keeping my bargain with the demon, who will doubtless this night consume the body of Amina in lieu of the one corpse that is still lacking. I resign myself to thy judgment, O Ahmed ben Becar, and I beseech thee for no other mercy than that of death, wherewith to terminate my double grief and my two-fold remorse.

When Noureddin Hassan had ended his narrative, the amazement of all who had heard him was verily multiplied, since no man could remember hearing a stranger tale. And the Cadi pondered for a long time and then gave judgment, saying:

"I must needs marvel at thy story, but the crimes thou hast committed are none the less heinous, and Iblis himself would stand aghast before them. However, some allowance must be made for the fact that thou hadst given thy word to the ghoul and wast bound as it were in honor to fulfill his demand, no matter how horrible its nature. And allowance must likewise be made for thy connubial grief which caused thee to forfend thy wife's body from the demon. Yet I cannot judge thee guiltless, though I know not the punishment which is merited in a case so utterly without parallel. Therefore, I set thee free, with this injunction, that thou shalt make atonement for thy crimes in the fashion that seemeth best to thee, and shalt render justice to thyself and to others in such degree as thou art able."

"I thank thee for this mercy," replied Noureddin Hassan; and he then withdrew from the court amid the wonderment of all who were present. There was much debate when he had gone, and many were prone to question the wisdom of the Cadi's decision. Some there were who maintained that Noureddin should have been sentenced to death without delay for his abominable actions though others argued for the sanctity of his oath to the ghoul, and would have exculpated him altogether or in part. And tales were told and instances were cited regarding the habits of ghouls and the strange plight of men who had surprised such demons in their nocturnal delvings. And again the discussion returned to Noureddin, and the judgment of the Cadi was once more upheld or assailed with divers arguments. But amid all this,

Ahmed ben Becar was silent, saying only:

"Wait, for this man will render justice to himself and to all others concerned, as far as the rendering thereof is possible."

So indeed it happened, for on the morning of the next day another body was found in the cemetery near Bussorah lying half-devoured on the grave of Noureddin Hassan's wife, Amina. And the body was that of Noureddin, self-slain, who in this manner had not only fulfilled the injunction of the Cadi but had also kept his bargain with the ghoul by providing the required number of corpses.

SOMETHING NEW

ell me something new," she moaned, twisting in his arms on the sofa. "Say or do something original — and I'll love you. Anything but the wheezy gags, the doddering compliments, the kisses that were stale before Antony passed them off on Cleopatra."

"Alas," he said, "there is nothing new in the world except the rose and gold and ivory of your perfect loveliness. And there is nothing original except my love for you."

"Old stuff," she sneered, moving away from him. "They all say that."

"They?" he queried, jealously.

"The ones before you, of course," she replied, in a tone of languid reminiscence. "It only took four lovers to convince me of the quotidian sameness of man. After that, I always knew what to expect. It was maddening: they came to remind me of so many cuckoo clocks, with the eternal monotony of their advances, the punctuality of their compliments. I soon knew the whole repertory. As for kissing — each one began with my hands, and ended with my lips. There was one genius, though, who kissed me on the throat the first time. I might have taken him, if he had lived up to the promise of such a beginning."

"What shall I say?" he queried, in despair. "Shall I tell you that your eyes are the unwaning moons above the cypress-guarded lakes of dreamland? Shall I say that your hair is colored like the sunsets of Cocaigne?"

She kicked off one of her slippers, with a little jerk of disgust.

"You aren't the first poet that I've had for a lover. One of them used to read me that sort of stuff by the hour. All about moons, and stars and sunsets, and rose-leaves

47

and lotus-petals."

"Ah," he cried hopefully, gazing at the slipperless foot. "Shall I stand on my head and kiss your tooty-wootsies?"

She smiled briefly. "That wouldn't be so bad. But you're not an acrobat, my dear. You'd fall over and break something — provided you didn't fall on me."

"Well, I give it up," he muttered, in a tone of hopeless resignation. "I've done my darndest to please you for the past four months; and I've been perfectly faithful and devoted, too; I haven't so much as looked corner-wise at another woman — not even that blue-eyed brunette who tried to vamp me at the Artists' Ball the other night."

She sighed impatiently. "What does that matter? I am sure you needn't be faithful unless you want to be. As for pleasing me — well, you did give a thrill once upon a time, during the first week of our acquaintance. Do you remember? We were lying out under the pines on the old rug that we had taken with us; and you suddenly turned to me and asked me if I would like to be a hamadryad . . . Ah! there is a hamadryad in every woman; but it takes a faun to call it forth . . . My dear, if you had only been a faun!"

"A real faun would have dragged you off by the hair," he growled, "So you wanted some of that caveman stuff, did you? I suppose that's what you mean by 'something new.'"

"Anything, anything, providing it is new," she drawled, with ineffable languor. Looking like a poem to Ennui by Baudelaire, she leaned back and lit another cigarette in her holder of carved ivory.

He look at her, and wondered if any one female had ever before hidden so much perversity, capriciousness, and incomprehensibility behind a rosebud skin and harvest-coloured hair. A sense of acute exasperation mounted in him — something that had smouldered for months, half-restrained by his natural instincts of chivalry and gentleness. He remembered an aphorism from Nietzsche: "When thou goest to women, take thy whip." "By Jove, the old boy had the right dope," he thought. "Too bad I didn't think to take my whip with me; but after all, I have my hands, and a little rough stuff can't make matters any worse."

Aloud, he said: "It's a pity no one ever thought to give you a good paddling. All women are spoiled and perverse, more or less, but you —" He broke off, and drew her across his knees like a naughty child, with a movement so muscular and sudden that she had neither the time nor the impulse to resist or cry out.

"I'm going to give you the spanking of your life," he growled, as his right hand rose and descended . . . The cigarette holder fell from her lips to the Turkish carpet, and began to burn a hole in the flowered pattern. . . . A dozen smart blows, with a sound like the clapping of shingles, and then he released her, and rose to his feet. His anger had vanished, and his only feeling was an overpowering sense of shame and consternation. He could merely wonder how and why he had done it.

"I suppose you will never forgive me," he began.

"Oh, you are wonderful," she breathed. "I didn't think you had it in you. My faun! My caveman! Do it again."

Doubly dumbfounded as he was, he had enough presence of mind to adjust himself to the situation. "Women are certainly the limit," he thought, dazedly. "But one must make the best of them, and miss no chances."

Preserving a grim and mysterious silence, he picked her up in his arms.

THE MALAY KRISE

ahib," said the sword-dealer, "this blade, which came from far Singapore, has not its equal for sharpness in all Delhi."

He handed me the blade for inspection. It was a long krise, or Malay knife, with a curious boat-shaped hilt, and, as he had said, was very keen.

"I bought it of Sidi Hassen, a Singapore dealer into whose possession it came at the sale of Sultan Sujah Ali's weapons and effects after the Sultan's capture by the British. Hast heard the tale, Sahib? No? It runs thus:

"Sujah Ali was the younger son of a great Sultan. There being little chance of his ever coming to the throne, he left his father's dominions, and becoming a pirate, set out to carve for himself a name and an empire. Though having at first but a few *prahus* (boats) and less than a hundred men, he made up this lack by his qualities of leadership, which brought him many victories, much plunder and considerable renown. His fame caused many men to join him, and his booty enabled him to build more *prahus*. Adding continually to his fleets, he soon swept the rivers of the Peninsula, and then began to venture upon the sea. In a few years his ships were held in fear and respect by every Dutch merchantman or Chinese junk whose sails loomed above the waters of the China Sea. Inland he began to overrun the dominions of the other Sultans, conquering, amongst others, that of his older brother, who had succeeded to his father's throne. Sujah Ali's fame reached far, and its shadow lay upon many peoples.

"Then the English came to the Peninsula and built Singapore. Sujah Ali despatched ships to prey upon their vessels, many of whom he succeeded in capturing. The English sent big ships after him, bearing many heavy guns and many armed men.

"The Sultan went to meet them in person, with the greater part of his fleet. It was a disastrous day for him. When the red sun sank into the sea, fully fifty of his best *prahus*, and thousands of his men, amongst whom he mourned several of his most noted captains, lay beneath the waters. He fled inland with the shattered remnant of his fleet.

"The British resolved to crush him decisively, sent boats up the rivers, and in numerous hard-fought battles they sank most of Sujah Ali's remaining *prahus*, and cleared land and water of the infesting pirates. The Sultan himself, however, they sought in vain. He had fled to a well-nigh inaccessible hiding-place — a small village deep in a network of creeks, swamps, and jungle-covered islands. Here he remained with a few fighting-men while the English hunted unsuccessfully for the narrow, winding entrances.

"Amina, his favorite wife, was among those who had accompanied him to this refuge. She was passionately attached to the Sultan, and, although such was his wish, had positively refused to be left behind.

"There was a beautiful girl in the village, with whom Sujah Ali became infatuated. He finally married her, and she exercised so great an influence over him that Amina, who had hitherto considered herself first in her husband's estimation, grew jealous. As time passed, and she perceived more clearly how complete was his infatuation, her jealousy grew more intense and violent, and at last prompted her to leave the village secretly one night, and to go to the captain of a British vessel which had been cruising up and down the river for weeks. To this man, one Rankling Sahib, she revealed the secret of Sujah Ali's hiding place. In thus betraying him, her desire was probably more for revenge upon her rival than upon the

Sultan.

"Rankling Sahib, guided by Amina, passed at midnight through the network of creeks and jungles. He landed his crew and entered the village. The Malays, taken completely by surprise, offered little or no resistance. Many awoke only to find themselves confronted by loaded rifles, and surrendered without opposition.

"Sujah Ali, who had lain awake all evening wondering as to the cause of Amina's absence, rushed out of his hut with half a score of his men, and made a futile attempt at escape. A desperate fight ensued, in which he used his krise, the same that thou seest, with deadly effect. Two of the English he stretched dead, and a third he wounded severely.

"Rankling Sahib had given orders that the Sultan be taken alive, if possible. Finally, wounded, weary and surrounded by his foes on all sides, the Sultan was made prisoner. And the next morning he was taken down the river to Singapore.

"This is the krise you see on the wall."

THE GHOST
OF MOHAMMED DIN

"I'll wager a hundred rupees that you won't stay there overnight," said Nicholson.

It was late in the afternoon, and we were seated on the veranda of my friend's bungalow in the Begum suburb at Hyderabad. Our conversation had turned to ghosts, on which subject I was, at the time, rather skeptical, and Nicholson, after relating a number of blood-curdling stories, had finished by remarking that a nearby house, which was said to be haunted, would give me an excellent chance to put the matter to the test.

"Done!" I answered, laughing.

"It's no joking matter," said my friend, seriously. "However, if you really wish to encounter the ghost, I can easily secure you the necessary permission. The house, a six-roomed bungalow, owned by one Yussuf Ali Borah, is tenanted only by the spirit who appears to regard it as his exclusive property.

"Two years ago it was occupied by a Moslem merchant named Mohammed Din, and his family and servants. One morning they found the merchant dead — stabbed through the heart, and no trace of his murderer, whose identity still remains unrevealed.

"Mohammed Din's people left, and the place was let to a Parsee up from Bombay on business. He vacated the premises abruptly about midnight, and told a wild tale the next morning of having encountered a number of disembodied spirits, describing the chief one as Mohammed Din.

"Several other people took the place in turn, but their occupancy was generally of short duration. All told tales similar to the Parsee's. Gradually it acquired a bad reputation, and the finding of tenants became impossible."

"Have you ever seen the ghost yourself?" I asked.

"Yes; I spent a night, or rather part of one, there, for I went out of the window about one o'clock. My nerves were not strong enough to stand it any longer. I wouldn't enter the place again for almost any sum of money."

Nicholson's story only confirmed my intention of occupying the haunted house. Armed with a firm disbelief in the supernatural, and a still firmer intention to prove it all rot, I felt myself equal to all the ghosts, native and otherwise, in India. Of my ability to solve the mystery, if there were any, I was quite assured.

"My friend," said Nicholson to Yussuf Ali Borah an hour later, "wishes to spend a night in your haunted bungalow."

The person addressed, a fat little Moslem gentleman, looked at me curiously.

"The house is at your service, Sahib," he said, "I presume that Nicholson Sahib has told you the experiences of the previous tenants?"

I replied that he had. "If the whole thing is not a trumped-up story, there is doubtless some trickery afoot," said I, "and I warn you that the trickster will not come off unharmed. I have a loaded revolver, and shall not hesitate to use it if I meet any disembodied spirits."

Yussuf's only answer was to shrug his shoulders.

He gave us the keys, and we set out for the bungalow, which was only a few minutes' walk distant. Night had fallen when we reached it. Nicholson unlocked the door and we entered, and lighting a lamp I had brought with me, set out on a tour of inspection. The furniture consisted chiefly of two charpoys, three tabourets, an old divan quite innocent of cushions, a broken punkah, a three-legged chair and a dilapidated rug. Everything was covered with dust; the shutters rattled disconsolately, and all the doors creaked. The other rooms were meagrely furnished. I could hear rats running about in the dark.

There was a compound adjoining, filled with rank reed and a solitary pipal tree. Nicholson said that the ghost generally appeared in one of the rooms opening upon it, and this I selected as the one in which to spend the night. It was a fitting place for ghosts to haunt. The ceiling sagged listlessly, and the one charpoy which it contained had a wobbly look.

"Sleep well," said Nicholson. "You will find the atmosphere of this spirit-ridden place most conducive to slumber."

"Rats!" said I.

"Yes, there are plenty of rats here," he answered as he went out.

Placing the lamp on a tabouret, I lay down, with some misgivings as to its stability, on the charpoy. Happily, these proved unfounded, and laying my revolver close at hand, I took out a newspaper and began to read.

Several hours passed and nothing unusual happened. The ghost failed to materialize, and about eleven, with my fine skepticism greatly strengthened, and feeling a trifle ashamed concerning the hundred rupees which my friend would have to hand over the next morning, I lay down and tried to go to sleep. I had no doubt that my threat about the revolver to Yussuf Ali Borah had checked any plans for scaring me that might have been entertained.

Scarcely were my eyes closed when all the doors and windows, which had been creaking and rattling all evening, took on renewed activity. A light breeze had sprung up, and one shutter, which hung only by a single hinge, began to drum a tune on the wall. The rats scuttled about with redoubled energy, and a particularly industrious fellow gnawed something in the further corner for about an hour. It was manifestly impossible to sleep. I seemed to hear whisperings in the air, and once thought that I detected faint footsteps going and coming through the empty rooms. A vague feeling of eeriness crept upon me, and it required a very strong mental effort to convince myself that these sounds were entirely due to imagination.

Finally the breeze died down, the loose shutter ceased to bang, the rat stopped gnawing, and comparative quiet being restored, I fell asleep. Two hours later I woke, and taking out my watch, saw, though the lamp had begun to burn dimly, that the hands pointed to two o'clock. I was about to turn over, when again I heard the mysterious footsteps, this time quite audibly. They seemed to approach my room, but when I judged them to be in the next apartment, ceased abruptly. I waited five minutes in a dead silence, with my nerves on edge and my scalp tingling.

Then I became aware that there was something between me and the opposite wall. At first it was a dim shadow, but as I watched, it darkened into a body. A sort of phosphorescent light emanated from it, surrounding it with pale radiance.

The lamp flared up and went out, but the figure was still visible. It was that of a tall native dressed in flowing white robes and a blue turban. He wore a bushy beard and had eyes like burning coals of fire. His gaze was directed intently upon me, and I felt cold shivers running up and down my spine. I wanted to shriek, but my tongue seemed glued to the roof of my mouth. The figure stepped forward and I noticed that the robe was red at the breast as though with blood.

This, then, was the ghost of Mohammed Din.

Nicholson's story was true, and for a moment my conviction that the supernatural was all nonsense went completely to pieces. Only momentarily, however, for I remembered that I had a revolver, and the thought gave me courage. Perhaps it was a trick after all, and anger arose in me, and a resolve not to let the trickster escape unscathed.

I raised the weapon with a quick movement and fired. The figure being not over five paces distant, it was impossible to miss, but when the smoke had cleared it had not changed its position.

It began to advance, making no sound, and in a few moments was beside the charpoy. With one remaining vestige of courage I raised my revolver and pulled the trigger three times in succession, but without visible effect. I hurled the weapon at the figure's head, and heard it crash against the opposite wall an instant later. The apparition, though visible, was without tangibility.

Now it began to disappear. Very slowly at first it faded, then more rapidly until I could make out only the bare outlines. Another instant and all was gone but the outline of one hand, which hung motionless in the air. I got up and made a step towards it, then stopped abruptly, for the outlines again began to fill in, the hand to darken and solidify. Now I noticed something I had not before seen — a heavy gold ring set with some green gem, probably an emerald, appeared to be on the middle finger.

The hand began to move slowly past me towards the door opening into the next apartment. Lighting the lamp, I followed, all fear being thrown aside and desiring to find the explanation of the phenomenon. I could hear faint footfalls beneath the hand, as though the owner, though invisible, were still present. I followed it through the adjoining apartment and into the next, where it again stopped and hung motionless. One finger was pointed toward the further corner, where stood a tabouret, or stand.

Impelled, I think, by some force other than my own volition, I went over and lifting the tabouret, found a small wooden box, covered with dust, beneath.

Turning about I saw that the hand had disappeared.

Taking the box with me, I returned to my room. The thing was made of very hard wood and in size was perhaps ten inches in length by eight in width and four in height. It was light, and the contents rustled when I shook it. I guessed them to be letters or papers, but having nothing to pry the box open with, I concluded to wait until morning before trying to.

Strange as it may seem, I soon fell asleep. You would naturally think that a man would not feel inclined to slumber immediately after encountering a disembodied spirit. I can give no explanation of it.

The sun was streaming through the window when I awoke, and so cheerful and matter-of-fact was the broad daylight that I wondered if the events of the night were not all a dream. The presence of the box, however, convinced me that they were not.

Nicholson came in and appeared much surprised and a trifle discomfited to find me still in possession.

"Well," he inquired, "what happened? What did you see?"

I told him what had occurred and produced the box as proof.

An hour afterwards, Nicholson, with a short native sword and considerable profanity, was trying to pry the thing open. He finally succeeded. Within were a number of closely-written sheets of paper and some letters, most of which were addressed to Mohammed Din.

The papers were mostly in the form of memoranda

and business accounts such as would be made by a merchant. They were written in execrable Urdu, hopelessly jumbled together, and though all were dated, it was no small task to sort them out. The letters were mostly regarding business affairs, but several, which were written in a very fair hand, were from a cousin of Mohammed Din's, one Ali Bagh, an Agra horse-trader. These, too, with one exception, were commonplace enough. Nicholson knitted his brows as he read it, and then handed it to me. The greater part, being of little interest, has escaped my memory, but I recollect that the last paragraph ran thus:

"I do not understand how you came by the knowledge, nor why you wish to use it to ruin me. It is all true. If you have any love for me, forbear."

"What does that mean?" asked Nicholson. "What secret did Mohammed Din possess that he could have used to ruin his cousin?"

We went through the memoranda carefully, and near the bottom found the following, dated April 21, 1881, according to our notation:

"Today I found the letters which I have long been seeking. They are ample proof of what I have long known, but have hitherto been unable to substantiate, that Ali Bagh is a counterfeiter, the chief of a large band. I have but to turn them over to the police, and he will be dragged away to jail, there to serve a term of many years. It will be good revenge — part compensation, at least, for the injuries he has done me."

"That explains Ali Bagh's letter," said Nicholson. "Mohammed Din was boastful enough to write to him, telling him that he knew of his guilt and intended to prove it."

Next were several sheets in a different hand and signed "Mallek Khan." Mallek Khan, it seemed, was a friend of Ali Bagh's, and the sheets were in the form of a letter. But being without fold, it was quite evident they had not been posted.

The communication related to certain counterfeiting schemes, and the names of a number of men implicated appeared. This, plainly, was the proof alluded to by Mohammed Din, and which he had threatened his cousin to turn over to the police.

There was nothing else of interest save the following in Mohammed Din's hand, dated April 17th, 1881:

"Tomorrow I shall give the papers to the authorities. I have delayed too long, and was very foolish to write to Ali Bagh.

"I passed a man in the street today who bore a resemblance to my cousin. . . . I could not be sure . . . But if he is here, then may Allah help me, for he will hesitate at nothing. . . ."

What followed was illegible.

"On the night of April 21st," said Nicholson, "Mohammed Din was killed by a person or persons unknown." He paused and then went on: "This Ali Bagh is a man with whom I have had some dealings in horses, and an especially vicious crook it was that he got three hundred rupees out of me for. He has a bad reputation as a horse-dealer, and the Agra police have long been patiently seeking evidence of his implication in several bold counterfeiting schemes. Mallek Khan, one of his accomplices, was arrested, tried and sentenced to fifteen years' imprisonment, but refused to turn State's evidence on Ali Bagh. The police are convinced that Ali Bagh was as much, if not more implicated, than Mallek Khan, but they can do nothing for lack of proof. The turning over of these papers, however, as poor Mohammed Din would have done had he lived, will lead to his arrest and conviction.

"It was Ali Bagh who killed Mohammed Din, I am morally convinced, his motive, of course, being to prevent the disclosure of his guilt. Your extraordinary experience last night and the murdered man's papers point to it. Yet we can prove nothing, and your tale would be laughed at in court."

Some blank sheets remained in the bottom of the box, and my friend tilted them out as he spoke. They fluttered to the veranda and something rolled out from amongst them and lay glittering in the sunshine. It was a heavy gold ring set with an emerald — the very same that I had seen upon the apparition's finger several hours before.

A week or so later, as the result of the papers that Nicholson sent to the Agra police, accompanied by an explanatory note, one Ali Bagh, horse-trader, found himself on trial, charged with counterfeiting. It was a very short trial, his character and reputation going badly against him, and it being proven that he was the leader of the gang of which Mallek Khan was thought to be a member, he was sentenced to a somewhat longer term in jail than his accomplice.

THE MIRROR IN
THE HALL OF EBONY

From the nethermost profound of slumber, from a gulf beyond the sun and stars that illume the Lethean shoals and the vague lands of somnolent visions, I floated on a black unrippling tide to the dark threshold of a dream. And in this dream I stood at the end of a long hall that was ceiled and floored and walled with black ebony, and was lit with a light that fell not from the sun or moon nor from any lamp. The hall was without doors or windows, and at the further extreme an oval mirror was framed in the wall. And standing there, I remembered nothing of all that had been; and the other dreams of sleep, and the dream of birth and of everything thereafter, were alike forgotten. And forgotten too was the name I had found among men, and the other names whereby the daughters of dream had known me; and memory was no older than my coming to that hall. But I wondered not, nor was I troubled thereby, and naught was strange to me: for the tide that had borne me to this threshold was the tide of Lethe.

Anon, though I knew not why, my feet were drawn adown the hall, and I approached the oval mirror. And in the mirror I beheld the haggard face that was mine, and the red mark on the cheek where one I loved had struck me in her anger, and the mark on the throat where her lips had kissed me in amorous devotion. And, seeing this, I remembered all that had been; and the other dreams of sleep, and the dream of birth and of everything thereafter, alike returned to me. And thus I recalled the name I had assumed beneath the terrene sun, and the names I had borne beneath the suns of sleep and of reverie. And I marvelled much, and was enormously troubled, and all things were most strange to me, and all things were as of yore.

THE MAHOUT

Arthur Merton, British resident at Jizapur, and his cousin, John Hawley, an Agra newspaper editor, who had run down into Central India for a few weeks' shooting at Merton's invitation, reined in their horses just outside the gates of Jizapur. The Maharajah's elephants, a score of the largest and finest "tuskers" in Central India, were being ridden out for their daily exercise. The procession was led by Rajah, the great elephant of State, who towered above the rest like a warship amongst merchantmen. He was a magnificent elephant, over twelve feet from his shoulders to the ground, and of a slightly lighter hue than the others, who were of the usual muddy gray. On the ends of his tusks gleamed golden knobs.

"What a kingly animal!" exclaimed Hawley, as Rajah passed.

As he spoke, the mahout, or driver, who had been sitting his charge like a bronze image, turned and met Hawley's eyes. He was a man to attract attention, this mahout, as distinctive a figure among his brother mahouts as was Rajah among the elephants. He was apparently very tall, and of a high-caste type, the eyes proud and fearless, the heavy beard carefully trimmed, and the face cast in a handsome, dignified mold.

Hawley gave a second exclamation as he met the mahout's gaze and stared at the man hard. The Hindu, after an impressive glance, turned his head, and the elephant went on.

"I could swear that I have seen that man before," said Hawley, at his cousin's interrogatory expression. "It was near Agra, about six years ago, when I was out riding one afternoon. My horse, a nervous, high-strung Waler, bolted at the sight of an umbrella which someone had left by the roadside. It was impossible to stop him, indeed, I had all I could to keep on. Suddenly, the Hindu we have just passed, or his double, stepped out into the road and grabbed the bridle. He was carried quite a distance, but managed to keep his grip, and the Waler finally condescended to stop. After receiving my thanks with a dignified deprecation of the service he had done me, the Hindu disappeared, and I have not seen him since." Hawley resumed, after a pause. "It is scarcely probable, though, that this mahout is the same. My rescuer was dressed as a high-caste, and it is not conceivable that such a one would turn elephant driver."

"I know nothing of the man," said Merton, as they rode on into the city. "He has been Rajah's mahout ever since I came here a year ago. Of course, as you say, he cannot be the man who stopped your horse. It is merely a chance resemblance."

The next afternoon, Hawley was out riding alone. He had left the main road for a smaller one running into the jungle, intending to visit a ruined temple of which Merton had told him. Suddenly he noticed elephant tracks in the dust, exceedingly large ones, which he concluded could have been made only by Rajah. A momentary curiosity as to why the elephant had been ridden off into the jungle, and also concerning the mahout, led Hawley to follow the tracks when the road branched and they took the path opposite to the one that he had intended to follow. In a few minutes he came to a spot of open ground in the thick luxuriant jungle, and reined in quickly at what he saw there.

Rajah stood in the clearing, holding something in his trunk which Hawley at first glance took to be a man, dressed in a blue and gold native attire, and with a red turban. Another look told him that it was merely a dummy — some old clothes stuffed with straw. As he watched, the mahout gave a low command, reinforced with a jab behind the ear from his ankus, or goad. Rajah gave an upward swing with his trunk, and released his hold on the figure, which flew skyward for at least twenty feet, and then dropped limply to earth. The mahout watched its fall with an expression of what seemed to be malevolence upon his face, though Hawley might have been mistaken as to this at the distance. He gave another command, and a jab at the elephant's cheek — a peculiar, quick thrust, at which Rajah picked the dummy up and placed it on his back behind the mahout in the place usually occupied by the howdah. The Hindu directing, the figure was again seized and hurled into the air.

Much mystified, Hawley watched several repetitions of this strange performance, but was unable to puzzle out what it meant. Finally, the mahout caught sight of him, and rode the elephant hastily away into the jungle on the opposite side of the clearing. Evidently he did not wish to be observed or questioned. Hawley continued his journey to the temple, thinking over the curious incident as he went. He did not see the mahout again that day.

He spoke of what he had seen to Merton that evening, but his cousin paid little attention to the tale, saying that no one could comprehend anything done by natives, and that it wasn't worth while to wonder at their actions anyway. Even if one could find the explanation, it wouldn't be worth knowing.

The scene in the jungle recurred to Hawley many times, probably because of the resemblance of the mahout to the man who had stopped his horse at Agra. But he could think of no plausible explanation of what he had seen. At last he dismissed the matter from his mind altogether.

At the time of Hawley's visit, great preparations were being made for the marriage of the Maharajah of Jizapur, Krishna Singh, to the daughter of the neighboring sovereign. There was to be much feasting, firing of guns, and a gorgeous procession. All the Rajahs, Ranas, and Thakurs, etc., for a radius of at least hundred miles, were to be present. The spectacle, indeed, was one of the inducements that had drawn Hawley down into Central India.

After two weeks of unprecedented activity and excitement in the city of Jizapur, the great day came, with incessant thunder of guns from the Maharajah's palace during all the forenoon, as the royalty of Central India arrived with its hordes of picturesque, tattered, dirty retainers and soldiery. Each king or dignitary was punctiliously saluted according to his rank, which in India is determined by the number of guns that may be fired in his honor.

At noon a great procession, the Maharajah heading it, issued from the palace to ride out and meet the bride and her father and attendants, who were to reach Jizapur at that hour.

Hawley and Merton watched the pageant from the large and many-colored crowd that lined the roadside without the city gates. As Rajah, the great State elephant, emerged, with Krishna Singh in the gold-embroidered howdah, or canopied seat, on his back, a rising cloud of dust in the distance proclaimed the coming of the bride and her relatives.

Behind the Maharajah came a number of elephants, bearing the nobles and dignitaries of Jizapur, and the neighboring princes. Then emerged richly caparisoned horses, with prismatically-attired riders — soldiers and attendants. Over this great glare of color and movement was the almost intolerable light of the midday Eastern sun.

The two Englishmen were some distance from the city gates, so that when the Maharajah's slow, majestic procession passed them, that of the bride was drawing near — a similar one, and less gorgeous only because it was smaller.

Perhaps fifty yards separated the two when something happened to bring both processions to a halt. Hawley, who happened at the moment to be idly watching the elephant Rajah, and his driver, saw the mahout reach swiftly forward and stab the animal's cheek with his goad, precisely as he had done on that day in the jungle when Hawley had come unexpectedly upon him. Probably no one else noticed the action, or, if they did, attached any importance to it in the excitement that followed.

As he had reached with his trunk for the dummy seated on his back, so Rajah reached into the howdah and grasped Krishna Singh about the waist. In an instant the astonished, terror-stricken Maharajah was dangling in mid-air where the elephant held him poised a moment. Then, in spite of the shouts, commands, and blows of his mahout, Rajah began to swing Krishna Singh to and fro, slowly at first, but with a gradually increasing speed. It was like watching a gigantic pendulum. The fascinated crowd gazed in a sudden and tense silence for what seemed to them hours, though they were really only seconds, before the elephant, with a last vicious upward impetus of his helpless victim, released his hold.

Krishna Singh soared skyward, a blot of gold and red against the intense, stark, blazing azure of the Indian sky. To the horror-stricken onlookers he seemed to hang there for hours, before he began to fall back from the height to which the giant elephant had tossed him as one would toss a tennis-ball. Hawley turned away, unable to look any longer, and in an instant heard the hollow, life-less thud as the body struck the ground.

The sound broke the spell of horror and amazement that had held the crowd, and a confused babble arose, interspersed with a few wails and cries. One sharp shriek came from the curtained howdah of the bride. The Maharajah's bodyguard at once galloped forward and formed a ring about the body. The crowd, to whom the elephant had gone "musth," or mad, began to retreat and disperse.

Hawley, in a few words, told his cousin of what he has seen the mahout do, and his belief that the elephant's action had thus been incited.

The two Englishmen went to the captain of the body-guard, who was standing by the side of the fallen Maha-rajah. Krishna Singh lay quite dead, his neck broken by the fall. The captain, upon being informed of what Hawley had seen, directed some of his men to go in search of the mahout, who, in the confusion, had slipped from Rajah's neck, disappearing no one knew where. Their search was unsuccessful, nor did a further one, con-tinued for over a week, reveal any trace of the elephant driver.

But several days afterward Hawley received a letter, bearing the Agra postmark. It was in a hand unfamiliar to him and was written in rather stiff, though perfectly cor-rect English, such as an educated native would write. It was as follows:

> To Hawley Sahib:
> I am the man who stopped the Sahib's horse near Agra one day, six years ago. Because I have seen in the Sahib's eyes that he recognized and remembers me, I am writing this. He will then understand much that has puzzled him.
> My father was Krishna Singh's half-brother.

Men who bore my father an enmity, invented evidence of a plot on his part to murder Krishna Singh and seize the throne. The Maharajah, bearing him little love and being of an intensely suspicious nature, required little proof to believe this, and caused my father and several others of the family to be seized and thrown into the palace dungeons. A few days later, without trial, they were led out and executed by the "Death of the Elephant." Perchance the Sahib has not heard of this. The manner of it is thus: The condemned man is made to kneel with his head on a block of stone, and an elephant, at a command from the driver, places one of his feet on the prisoner's head, killing him, of course, instantly.

I, who was but a youth at the time, by some inadvertence was allowed to escape, and made my way to Agra, where I remained several years with distant relatives, learning, in that time, to speak and write English I was intending to enter the service of the British Raj, when an idea of revenge on Krishna Singh, for my father's death, suddenly sprang into full conception. I had long plotted, forming many impracticable and futile plans for vengeance, but the one that then occurred to me seemed possible, though extremely difficult. As the Sahib has seen, it proved successful.

I at once left Agra, disguising myself as a low-caste, and went to Burma, where I learned elephant-driving — a work not easy for one who has not been trained to it from boyhood. In doing this, I sacrificed my caste. In my thirst for revenge, however, it seemed but a little thing.

After four years in the jungle I came to Jizapur and, being a skilled and fully accredited mahout, was given a position in the Maharajah's stables. Krishna Singh never suspected my identity, for I had changed greatly in the ten years since I had fled from Jizapur, and who would have thought to find Kshatriya in the position of such a low-caste elephant-driver?

Gradually, for my skill and trustworthiness, I was advanced in position, and at last was entrusted with the State elephant, Rajab. This was what I had long been aiming at, for on my attaining the care of Krishna Singh's own elephant depended the success or failure of my plan.

This position obtained, my purpose was but half-achieved. It was necessary that the elephant be trained for his part, and this, indeed, was perhaps the most difficult and dangerous pact of my work. It was not easy to avoid observation, and detection was likely to prove fatal to me and to my plan. On that day when the Sahib came upon me in the jungle, I thought my scheme doomed, and prepared to flee. But evidently no idea of the meaning of the performance in the jungle entered the Sahib's mind.

At last came my day of revenge, and after the Maharajah's death I succeeded in miraculously escaping, though I had fully expected to pay for my vengeance with my own life. I am safe now — not all the police and secret emissaries in India can find me.

The death that my father met has been visited upon his murderer, and the shadow of those dreadful days and of that unavenged crime has at last been lifted from my heart. I go forth content, to face life and fate calmly, and with a mind free and untroubled.

THE PRIMAL CITY

In these after-days, when all things are touched with in-soluble doubt, I am not sure of the purpose that had taken us into that little-visited land. I recall, however, that we had found explicit mention, in a volume of which we possessed the one existing copy, of certain vast primordial ruins lying amid the bare plateaus and stark pinnacles of the region. How we had acquired the volume I do not remember: but Sebastian Polder and I had given our youth and manhood to the quest of hidden knowledge; and this book was a compendium of all things that men have forgotten or ignored in their desire to repudiate the inexplicable.

We, being enamoured of mystery, and seeking ever for the clues that material science has disregarded, pondered much upon these pages written in an antique alphabet. The location of the ruins was clearly stated, though in terms of an obsolete geography; and I remember our excitement when we had marked the position on a terrestrial globe. We were consumed by a wild eagerness to visit the alien city. Perhaps we wished to verify a strange and fearful theory which we had formed regarding the nature of the earth's primal inhabitants; perhaps we sought to recover the buried records of a lost science . . . or perhaps there was some other and darker objective. . . .

I recall nothing of the first stages of our journey, which must have been long and arduous. But I recall distinctly that we travelled for many days amid the bleak, treeless uplands that rose like a many-tiered embankment towards the range of high pyramidal summits guarding the secret city. Our guide was a native of the country, sodden and taciturn, with intelligence little above that of the llamas who carried our supplies. But we had been assured that he knew the way to the ruins, which had long been forgotten by most of his fellow-countrymen. Rare and scant was the local legendry regarding the place and its builders; and, after many queries, we could add nothing to the knowledge gained from the immemorial volume, The city, it seemed, was nameless; and the region about it was untrodden by man.

Desire and curiosity raged within us like a calenture; and we heeded little the hazards and travails of our journey. Over us stood the eternally vacant heavens, matching the vacant landscape. The route steepened; and above us now was a wilderness of cragged and chasmed rock, where nothing dwelt but the sinister wide-winged condors.

Often we lost sight of certain eminent peaks that had served us for landmarks. But it seemed that our guide knew the way, as if led by an instinct more subtle than memory or intelligence; and at no time did he hesitate. At intervals we came to the broken fragments of a paved road that had formerly traversed the whole of this rugged region: broad cyclopean blocks of gneiss, channelled as if by the storms of cycles older than human history. And in some of the deeper chasms we saw the eroded piers of great bridges that had spanned them in other time. These ruins reassured us; for in the primordial volume there was mention of a highway and of mighty bridges, leading to the fabulous city.

Polder and I were exultant; and yet we both shivered with a curious terror when we tried to read certain inscriptions that were still deeply engraved on the worn stones. No living man, though erudite in all the tongues of Earth, could have deciphered those characters; and perhaps it was their very alienage that frightened us. We had sought diligently during many years for all that transcends the dead level of mortality through age or remoteness or strangeness; we had longed for the elder and darker secrets: but such longing was not incompatible with fear. Better than those who had walked always in the common paths, we knew the perils that might attend our exorbitant and solitary researches.

Often we had debated, with variously fantastic conjectures, the enigma of the mountain-builded city. But towards our journey's end, when the vestiges of that pristine people multiplied around us, we fell into long periods of silence, sharing the taciturnity of our stolid guide, Thoughts came to us that were overly strange for utterance; the chill of elder eons entered our hearts from the ruins — and did not depart.

We toiled on between the desolate rocks and the sterile heavens, breathing an air that became thin and painful to the lungs, as if from some admixture of cosmic ether. At high noon we reached an open pass, and saw before us, at the end of a long and vertiginous perspective, the city that had been described as an unnamed ruin in a volume antedating all other known books.

The place was built on an inner peak of the range, surrounded by snowless summits little sterner and loftier than itself. On one side the peak fell in a thousand-foot precipice from the overhanging ramparts; on another, it was terraced with wild cliffs; but the third side, flung towards us, was no more than a steep and broken acclivity. The rock of the whole mountain was strangely ruinous and black; but the city walls, though equally worn and riven, were conspicuous above it at a distance of leagues, being plainly of megalithic vastness.

Polder and I beheld the bourn of our worldwide search with unvoiced thoughts and emotions. The Indian made no comment, pointing impassively towards the far summit with its crown of ruins. We hurried on, wishing to complete our journey by daylight; and, after plunging into an abysmal valley, we began at mid-afternoon the ascent of the slope towards the city.

It was like climbing amid the overthrown and fire-blasted blocks of a titan citadel. Everywhere the slope was rent into huge, obliquely angled masses, often partly vitrified. Plainly, at some former time, it had been subjected to the action of intense heat; and yet there were no volcanic craters in that vicinity. I felt a vague sense of awe and terror, as I recalled a passage in the old volume, hinting ambiguously at the fate that had long ago destroyed the city's inhabitants:

"For the people of that city had reared its walls and towers too high amid the region of the clouds; and the clouds came down in their anger and smote the city with dreadful fires; and thereafter the place was peopled no more by those primal giants who had built it, but had only the clouds for inhabitants and custodians."

We had left our three llamas at the slope's bottom, merely taking with us provisions for one night. Thus, unhampered, we made fair progress in spite of the ever-varying obstacles offered by the shattered scarps. After a while we came to the hewn steps of a stairway mounting towards the summit; but the steps had been wrought for the feet of colossi, and, in many places, were part of the heaved and tilted ruin; so they did not greatly facilitate our climbing.

The sun was still high above western pass behind us; and I was surprised, as we went on, by a sudden deepening of the charlike blackness on the rocks. Turning, I saw that several greyish vapoury masses, which might have been either clouds or smoke, were drifting about the summits that overlooked the pass; and one of these masses, rearing like a limbless figure, upright and colossal, had interposed itself between us and the sun.

I called the attention of my companions to this phenomenon; for clouds were almost unheard-of amid those arid mountains in summer; and the presence of smoke would have been equally hard to explain. Moreover, the grey masses were different from any cloud-forms we had ever seen. They possessed a peculiar capacity and sharpness of outline, a baffling suggestion of weight and solidity. Moving sluggishly into the heavens above the pass, they preserved their original contours and their separateness. They seemed to swell and tower, coming towards us on the blue air from which, as yet, no lightest breath of wind had reached us. Floating thus, they maintained the erectness of massive columns or of giants marching on a plain.

I think we all felt an alarm that was none the less urgent for its vagueness. Somehow, from that instant, it seemed that we were penned up by unknown powers and were cut off from all possibility of retreat. All at once, the dim legends of the ancient volume had assumed a menacing reality, We had ventured into a place of hidden peril — and the peril was upon us. In the movement of the clouds there was something alert, deliberate and implacable. Polder spoke with a sort of horror in his voice, uttering the thought that had already occurred to me:

"They are the sentinels who guard this region — and they have espied us!"

We heard a harsh cry from the Indian, who stood gazing and pointing upwards. Several of the unnatural cloud-shapes had appeared on the summit towards which we were climbing, above the megalithic ruins. Some arose half-hidden by the walls, as if from behind a breast-work; others stood, as it were, on the topmost towers and battlements, bulking in portentous menace, like the cumuli of a thunderstorm.

Then, with terrifying swiftness, many more of the

cloud-presences towered from the four quarters, emerging from behind the great peaks or assuming sudden visibility in mid-air. With equal and effortless speed, as if convoked by an unheard command, they gathered in converging lines up the eyrielike ruins. We, the climbers, and the whole slope about us and the valley below, were plunged in a twilight cast by the clouds.

The air was still windless, but it weighed upon us as if burdened with the wings of a thousand evil demons. We were overwhelmingly conscious of our exposed position, for we had paused on a wide landing of the mountain-hewn steps. We could have concealed ourselves amid the huge fragments on the slope; but, for the nonce, we were too exhausted to be capable of the simplest movement, The rarity of the air had left us weak and gasping. And the chill of altitude crept into us.

In a close-ranged army, the clouds mustered above and around us. They rose into the very zenith, swelling to insuperable vastness, and darkening like Tartarean gods. The sun had disappeared, leaving no faintest beam to prove that it still hung unfallen and undestroyed in the heavens.

I felt that I was crushed into the very stone by the eyeless regard of that awful assemblage, judging and condemning us. We had, I thought, trespassed upon a region conquered long ago by strange elemental entities and forbidden henceforward to man. We had approached their very citadel; and now we must meet the doom our rashness had invited. Such thoughts, like a black lightning, flared in my brain, even as my logic tried to analyse the reason for the thoughts.

Now, for the first time, I became aware of sound, if the word can be applied to a sensation so anomalous. It was as if the oppression that weighed upon me had become audible; as if palpable thunders poured over and past me. I felt and heard them in every nerve, and they roared through my brain like torrents from the opened floodgates of some tremendous weir in a world of genii.

Downwards upon us, with limbless Atlantean stridings, there swept the cloudy cohorts. Their swiftness was that of mountain-sweeping winds. The air was riven as if by the tumult of a thousand tempests, was rife with an unmeasured elemental malignity. I recall but partially the events that ensued; but the impression of insufferable darkness, of demonic clamour and trampling, and the pressure of thunderous onset, remains forever indelible. Also, there were voices that called out with the stridor of clarions in a war of gods, uttering ominous syllables, that man's ear could never seize.

Before those vengeful shapes, we could not stand for an instant. We hurled ourselves madly down the shadowed steps of the giant stairs. Polder and the guide were a little ahead of me, and I saw them in that baleful twilight through sheets of sudden rain, on the verge of a deep chasm, which, in our ascent, had compelled us to much circumambulation. I saw them fall together — and yet I swear that they did not fall into the chasm: for one of the clouds was upon them, whirling over them, even as they fell. There was a fusion as of forms beheld in delirium. For an instant the two men were like vapours that swelled and swirled, towering high as the cloud that had covered them; and the cloud itself was a misty Janus, with two heads and bodies, melting into its column . . .

After that I remember nothing more except the sense of vertiginous falling. By some miracle I must have reached the edge of the chasm and flung myself into its depths without being overtaken as the others had been. How I escaped is forevermore an enigma.

When I returned to awareness, stars were peering down like chill incurious eyes between black and jagged lips of rock. The air had turned sharp with nightfall in a mountain land. My body ached with a hundred bruises and my right forearm was limp and useless when I tried to raise myself. A dark mist of horror stifled my thoughts. Struggling to my feet with pain-racked effort, I called aloud, though I knew that none would answer me. Then, striking match after match, I searched the chasm and found myself, as I had expected, alone. Nowhere was there any trace of my companions: they had vanished utterly as clouds vanish.

Somehow, by night, with a broken arm, I climbed from the steep fissure. I must have made my way down the frightful mountainside and out of that namelessly haunted and guarded land. I remember that the sky was clear, that the stars were undimmed by any semblance of cloud; and that somewhere in the valley I found one of our llamas, still laden with its stock of provisions.

Plainly I was not pursued by the clouds. Perhaps they were concerned only with the warding of that mysterious primal city from human intrusion. Some day I shall learn their true nature and entity, and the secret of those ruinous walls and crumbling keeps, and the fate of my companions. But still, through my nightly dreams and diurnal visions, the dark shapes move with the tumult and thunder of a thousand storms; my soul is crushed into the earth with the burden of fear, and they pass over me with the speed and vastness of vengeful gods; and I hear their voices calling like clarions in the sky, with ominous, world-shaking syllables that the ear can never seize.

THE HUNTERS FROM BEYOND

I have seldom been able to resist the allurement of a bookstore, particularly one that is well supplied with rare and exotic items. Therefore I turned in at Toleman's to browse around for a few minutes. I had come to San Francisco for one of my brief, biannual visits, and had started early that idle forenoon to an appointment with Cyprian Sincaul, the sculptor, a second or third cousin of mine, whom I had not seen for several years.

The studio was only a block from Toleman's, and there seemed to be no especial object in reaching it ahead of time. Cyprian had offered to show me his collection of recent sculptures; but, remembering the smooth mediocrity of his former work, amid which were a few banal efforts to achieve horror and grotesquerie, I did not anticipate anything more than an hour or two of dismal boredom.

The little shop was empty of customers. Knowing my proclivities, the owner and his one assistant became tacitly non-attentive after a word of recognition, and left me to rummage at will among the curiously laden shelves. Wedged in between other but less alluring titles, I found a deluxe edition of Goya's "Proverbios." I began to turn the heavy pages, and was soon engrossed in the diabolic art of these nightmare-nurtured drawings.

It has always been incomprehensible to me that I did not shriek aloud with mindless, overmastering terror, when I happened to look up from the volume, and saw the thing that was crouching in a corner of the bookshelves before me. I could not have been more hideously startled if some hellish conception of Goya had suddenly come to life and emerged from one of the pictures in the folio.

What I saw was a forward-slouching, vermin-gray figure, wholly devoid of hair or down or bristles, but marked with faint, etiolated rings like those of a serpent that has lived in darkness. It possessed the head and brow of an anthropoid ape, a semi-canine mouth and jaw, and arms ending in twisted hands whose black hyena talons nearly scraped the floor. The thing was infinitely bestial, and, at the same time, macabre; for its parchment skin was shriveled, corpselike, mummified, in a manner impossible to convey; and from eye sockets well-nigh deep as those of a skull, there glimmered evil slits of yellowish phosphorescence, like burning sulphur. Fangs that were stained as if with poison or gangrene, issued from the slavering, half-open mouth; and the whole attitude of the creature was that of some maleficent monster in readiness to spring.

Though I had been for years a professional writer of stories that often dealt with occult phenomena, with the weird and the spectral, I was not at this time possessed of any clear and settled belief regarding such phenomena. I had never before seen anything that I could identify as a phantom, nor even an hallucination; and I should hardly have said offhand that a bookstore on a busy street, in full summer daylight, was the likeliest of places in which to see one. But the thing before me was assuredly nothing that could ever exist among the permissible forms of a sane world. It was too horrific, too atrocious, to be anything but a creation of unreality.

Even as I stared across the Goya, sick with a half-incredulous fear, the apparition moved toward me. I say that it moved, but its change of position was so instantaneous, so utterly without effort or visible transition, that the verb is hopelessly inadequate. The foul specter had seemed five or six feet away. But now it was stooping directly above the volume that I still held in my hands, with its loathsomely lambent eyes peering upward at my face, and a gray-green slime drooling from its mouth on the broad pages. At the same time I breathed an insupportable fetor, like a mingling of rancid serpent-stench with the moldiness of antique charnels and the fearsome reek of newly decaying carrion.

In a frozen timelessness that was perhaps no more than a second or two, my heart appeared to suspend its beating, while I beheld the ghastly face. Gasping, I let the Goya drop with a resonant bang on the floor, and even as it fell, I saw that the vision had vanished.

Toleman, a tonsured gnome with shell-rimmed goggles, rushed forward to retrieve the fallen volume, exclaiming: "What is wrong, Mr. Hastane? Are you ill?" From the meticulousness with which he examined the binding in search of possible damage, I knew that his chief solicitude was concerning the Goya. It was plain that neither he nor his clerk had seen the phantom; nor could I detect aught in their demeanor to indicate that they had noticed the mephitic odor that still lingered in the air like an exhalation from broken graves. And, as far as I could tell, they did not even perceive the grayish slime that still polluted the open folio.

I do not remember how I managed to make my exit from the shop. My mind had become a seething blur of muddled horror, of crawling, sick revulsion from the supernatural vileness I had beheld, together with the direst apprehension for my own sanity and safety. I recall only that I found myself on the street above Toleman's, walking with feverish rapidity toward my cousin's studio, with a neat parcel containing the Goya volume under my arm. Evidently, in an effort to atone for ny clumsiness, I must have bought and paid for the book by a sort of automatic impulse, without any real awareness of what I was doing.

I came to the building in which was my destination, but went on around the block several times before entering. All the while I fought desperately to regain my self-control and equipoise. I remember how difficult it was even to moderate the pace at which I was walking, or refrain from breaking into a run; for it seemed to me that I was fleeing all the time from an invisible pursuer. I tried to argue with myself, to convince the rational part of my mind that the apparition had been the product of some evanescent trick of light and shade, or a temporary dimming of eyesight. But such sophistries were useless; for I had seen the gargoylish terror all too distinctly, in an unforgettable fullness of grisly detail.

What could the thing mean? I had never used narcotic drugs or abused alcohol. My nerves, as far as I knew, were in sound condition. But either I had suffered a visual hallucination that might mark the beginning of some obscure cerebral disorder, or had been visited by a spectral phenomenon, by something from realms and dimensions that are past the normal scope of human perception. It was a problem either for the alienist or the occultist.

Though I was still damnably upset, I contrived to regain a nominal composure of my faculties. Also, it occurred to me that the unimaginative portrait busts and tamely symbolic figure-groups of Cyprian Sincaul might serve admirably to sooth my shaken nerves. Even his grotesques would seem sane and ordinary by comparison with the blasphemous gargoyle that had drooled before me in the bookshop.

I entered the studio building, and climbed a worn stairway to the second floor, where Cyprian had established himself in a somewhat capacious suite of rooms. As I went up the stairs, I had the peculiar feeling that somebody was climbing them just ahead of me; but I could neither see nor hear anyone, and the hall above was no less silent and empty than the stairs.

Cyprian was in his atelier when I knocked. After an interval which seemed unduly long, I heard him call out, telling me to enter. I found him wiping his hands on an old cloth, and surmised that he had been modeling. A sheet of light burlap had been thrown over what was plainly an ambitious but unfinished group of figures, which occupied the center of the long room. All around were other sculptures, in clay, bronze, marble, and even the terra-cotta and steatite which he sometimes employed for his less conventional conceptions. At one end of the room there stood a heavy Chinese screen.

At a single glance I realized that a great change had occurred, both in Cyprian Sincaul and his work. I remembered him as an amiable, somewhat flabby-looking youth, always dapperly dressed, with no trace of the dreamer or visionary. It was hard to recognize him now, for he had become lean, harsh, vehement, with an air of pride and penetration that was almost Luciferian. His unkempt mane of hair was already shot with white, and his eyes were electrically brilliant with a strange knowledge, and yet somehow were vaguely furtive, as if there dwelt behind them a morbid and macabre fear.

The change in his sculpture was no less striking. The respectable tameness and polished mediocrity were gone, and in their place, incredibly, was something little short of genius. More unbelievable still, in view of the laboriously ordinary grotesques of his earlier phase, was the trend that his art had now taken. All around me were frenetic, murderous demons, satyrs mad with nympholepsy, ghouls that seemed to sniff the odors of the charnel, lamias voluptuously coiled about their victims, and less nameable things that belonged to the outland realms of evil myth and malign superstition.

Sin, horror, blasphemy, diablerie — the lust and malice of pandemonium — all had been caught with impeccable art. The potent nightmarishness of these creations was not calculated to reassure my trembling nerves; and all at once I felt an imperative desire to escape from the studio, to flee from the baleful throng of frozen cacodemons and chiseled chimeras.

My expression must have betrayed my feelings to some extent.

"Pretty strong work, aren't they?" said Cyprian, in a loud, vibrant voice, with a note of harsh pride and triumph. "I can see that you are surprised — you didn't look for anything of the sort, I dare say."

"No, candidly, I didn't," I admitted. "Good Lord, man, you will become the Michelangelo of diabolism if you go on at this rate. Where on Earth do you get such stuff?"

"Yes, I've gone pretty far," said Cyprian, seeming to disregard my question. "Further even than you think, probably. If you could know what I know, could see what I have seen, you might make something really worthwhile out of your weird fiction, Philip. You are very clever and imaginative, of course. But you've never had any experience."

I was startled and puzzled. "Experience? What do you mean?"

"Precisely that. You try to depict the occult and the supernatural without even the most rudimentary first-hand knowledge of them. I tried to do something of the same sort in sculpture, years ago, without knowledge; and doubtless you recall the mediocre mess that I made of it, But I've learned a thing or two since then."

"Sounds as if you had made the traditional bond with the devil, or something of the sort," I observed, with a feeble and perfunctory levity.

Cyprian's eyes narrowed slightly, with a strange, secret look.

"I know what I know. Never mind how or why. The world in which we live isn't the only world; and some of the others lie closer at hand than you think. The boundaries of the seen and the unseen are sometimes interchangeable."

Recalling the malevolent phantom, I felt a peculiar disquietude as I listened to his words. An hour before, his statement would have impressed me as mere theorizing, but now it assumed an ominous and terrifying significance.

"What makes you think I have had no experience of the occult?" I asked.

"Your stories hardly show anything of the kind — anything factual or personal. They are all palpably made up. When you've argued with a ghost, or watched the ghouls at mealtime, or fought with an incubus, or suckled a vampire, you may achieve some genuine characterization and color along such lines."

For reasons that should be fairly obvious, I had not intended to tell anyone of the unbelievable thing at Toleman's. Now, with a singular mixture of emotions, of compulsive, eery terrors aad desire to refute the animadversions of Cyprian, I found myself describing the phantom.

He listened with an inexpressive look, as if his thoughts were occupied with other matters than my story. Then, when I had finished:

"You are becoming more psychic than I imagined. Was your apparition anything like one of these?"

With the last words, he lifted the sheet of burlap from the muffled group of figures beside which he had been standing.

I cried out involuntarily with the shock of that appalling revelation, and almost tottered as I stepped back.

Before me, in a monstrous semicircle, were seven
creatures who might all have been modeled from the gargoyle that had confronted me across the folio of Goya
drawings. Even in several that were still amorphous or
incomplete, Cyprian had conveyed with a damnable art
the peculiar mingling of primal bestiality and mortuary
putrescence that had signalized the phantom. The seven
monsters had closed in on a cowering, naked girl, and
were all clutching foully toward her with their hyena
claws. The stark, frantic, insane terror on the face of the
girl, and the slavering hunger of her assailants, were
alike unbearable. The group was a masterpiece, in its
consummate power of technique — but a masterpiece
that inspired loathing rather than admiration. And following my recent experience, the sight of it affected me
with indescribable alarm. It seemed to me that I had gone
astray from the normal, familiar world into a land of
detestable mystery, of prodigious and unnatural menace.

Held by an abhorrent fascination, it was hard for me
to wrench my eyes away from the figure-piece. At last I
turned from it to Cyprian himself. He was regarding me
with a cryptic air, beneath which I suspected a covert
gloating.

"How do you like my little pets?" he inquired. "I am
going to call the composition 'The Hunters from Beyond.'"

Before I could answer, a woman suddenly appeared
from behind the Chinese screen. I saw that she was the
model for the girl in the unfinished group. Evidently she
had been dressing, and she was now ready to leave, for
she wore a tailored suit and a smart toque. She was beautiful, in a dark, semi-Latin fashion; but her mouth was
sullen and reluctant, and her wide, liquid eyes were wells

of strange terror as she gazed at Cyprian, myself, and the uncovered statue-piece.

Cyprian did not introduce me. He and the girl talked together in low tones for a minute or two, and I was unable to overhear more than half of what they said. I gathered, however, that an appointment was being made for the next sitting. There was a pleading, frightened note in the girl's voice, together with an almost maternal concern; and Cyprian seemed to be arguing with her or trying to reassure her about something. At last she went out, with a queer, supplicative glance at me — a glance whose meaning I could only surmise and could not wholly fathom.

"That was Marta," said Cyprian. "She is half Irish, half Italian. A good model; but my new sculptures seem to be making her a little nervous." He laughed abruptly, with a mirthless, jarring note that was like the cachinnation of a sorcerer.

"In God's name, what are you trying to do here?" I burst out. "What does it all mean? Do such abominations really exist, on earth or in any hell?"

He laughed again, with an evil subtlety, and became evasive all at once. "Anything may exist, in a boundless universe with multiple dimensions. Anything may be real — or unreal. Who knows? It is not for me to say. Figure it out for yourself, if you can — there's a vast field for speculation — and perhaps for more than speculation."

With this, he began immediately to talk of other topics. Baffled, mystified, with a sorely troubled mind and nerves that were more unstrung than ever by the black enigma of it all, I ceased to question him. Simultaneously, my desire to leave the studio became almost overwhelming — a mindless, whirlwind panic that prompted me to run pell-mell from the room and down the stairs into the wholesome normality of the common, twentieth century streets. It seemed to me that the rays which fell through the skylight were not those of the sun, but of some darker orb; that the room was touched with unclean webs of shadow where shadow should not have been; that the stone Satans, the bronze lamias, the terracotta satyrs, and the clay gargoyles had somehow increased in number and might spring to malignant life at any instant.

Hardly knowing what I said, I continued to converse for a while with Cyprian. Then, excusing myself on the score of a nonexistent luncheon appointment, and promising vaguely to return for another visit before my departure from the city, I took my leave.

I was surprised to find my cousin's model in the lower hall, at the foot of the stairway. From her manner, and her first words, it was plain that she had been waiting.

"You are Mr. Philip Hastane, aren't you?" she said, in an eager, agitated voice. "I am Marta Fitzgerald. Cyprian has often mentioned you, and I believe that he admires you a lot. Maybe you'll think me crazy, but I had to speak to you. I can't stand the way that things are going here, and I'd refuse to come to the place any more, if it wasn't that I — like Cyprian so much.

"I don't know what he has done — but he is altogether different from what he used to be. His new work is so horrible — you can't imagine how it frightens me. The sculptures he does are more hideous, more hellish all the time. Ugh! those drooling, dead-gray monsters in that new group of his — I can hardly bear to be in the studio with them. It isn't right for anyone to depict such things. Don't you think they are awful, Mr. Hastane? They look as if they had broken loose from hell — and make you think that hell can't be very far away. It is wrong and wicked for anyone to — even imagine them; and I wish that Cyprian would stop. I am afraid that something will happen to him — to his mind — if he goes on. And I'll go mad, too, if I have to see those monsters many more times. My God! No one could keep sane in that studio."

She paused, and appeared to hesitate. Then:

"Can't you do something, Mr. Hastane! Can't you talk to him, and tell him how wrong it is, and how dangerous to his mental health? You must have a lot of influence with Cyprian — you are his cousin, aren't you? And he thinks you are very clever, too. I wouldn't ask you, if I hadn't been forced to notice so many things that aren't as they should be.

"I wouldn't bother you, either, if I knew anyone else to ask. He has shut himself up in that awful studio for the past year, and he hardly ever sees anybody. You are the first person that he has invited to see his new sculptures. He wants them to be a complete surprise for the critics and the public, when he holds his next exhibition.

"But you'll speak to Cyprian, won't you, Mr. Hastane? I can't do anything to stop him — he seems to exult in the mad horrors he creates. And he merely laughs at me when I try to tell him the danger. However, I think that those things are making him a little nervous sometimes — that he is growing afraid of his own morbid imagination. Perhaps he will listen to you."

If I had needed anything more to unnerve me, the desperate pleading of the girl and her dark, obscurely baleful hintings would have been enough. I could see that she loved Cyprian, that she was frantically anxious concerning him, and hysterically afraid; otherwise, she would not have approached an utter stranger in this fashion.

"But I haven't any influence with Cyprian," I protested, feeling a queer embarrassment. "And what am I to say to him? His new sculptures are magnificent — I have never seen anything more powerful of the kind. And how could I advise him to stop doing them? There would be no legitimate reason; he would simply laugh me out of the studio. An artist has the right to choose his own sub-ject-matter, even if he takes it from the nether pits of Limbo and Erebus."

The girl must have pleaded and argued with me for many minutes in that deserted hall. Listening to her, and trying to convince her of my inability to fulfil her request, was like a dialog in some futile and tedious nightmare. During the course of it, she told me a few details that I am unwilling to record in this narrative; details that were too morbid and too shocking for belief, regarding the mental alteration of Cyprian, and his new subject-matter and method of work. There were direct and oblique hints of a growing perversion; but somehow it seemed that much more was being held back; that even in her most horri-fying disclosures she was not wholly frank with me. At last, with some sort of hazy promise that I would speak to Cyprian, would remonstrate with him, I succeeded in getting away from her, and returned to my hotel.

The afternoon and evening that followed were tinged as by the tyrannous adumbration of an ill dream. I felt that I had stepped from the solid earth into a gulf of seething, menacing, madness-haunted shadow, and was lost henceforward to all rightful sense of location or di-rection. It was all too hideous — and too doubtful and unreal. The change in Cyprian himself was no less bewil-dering, and hardly less horrifying, than the vile phantom of the bookshop, and the demon sculptures that dis-played a magisterial art. It was as if the man had become possessed by some satanic energy or entity.

Everywhere that I went, I was powerless to shake off

the feeling of an intangible pursuit, of a frightful, unseen vigilance. It seemed to me that the worm-gray face and sulphurous eyes would reappear at any moment; that the semicanine mouth with its gangrene-dripping fangs might come to slaver above the restaurant table at which I ate, or upon the pillow of my bed. I did not dare to reopen the purchased Goya volume, for fear of finding that certain pages were still defiled with a spectral slime.

I went out and spent the evening in cafés, in theaters, wherever people thronged and lights were bright. It was after midnight when I finally ventured to brave the solitude of my hotel bedroom. Then there were endless hours of nerve-wrung insomnia, of shivering, sweating apprehension beneath the electric bulb that I had left burning. Finally, a little before dawn, by no conscious transition and with no premonitory drowsiness, I fell asleep.

I remember no dreams — only the vast, incubuslike oppression that persisted even in the depth of slumber, as if to drag me down with its formless, ever-clinging weight into gulfs beyond the reach of created flight or the fathoming of organized entity.

It was almost noon when I awoke, and found myself staring into the verminous, apish, mummy-dead face and hell-illumined eyes of the gargoyle that had crouched before me in the corner at Toleman's. The thing was standing at the foot of my bed; and behind it as I stared, the wall of the room, which was covered with a floral paper, dissolved in an infinite vista of grayness, teeming with ghoulish forms that emerged like monstrous, misshapen bubbles from plains of undulant ooze and skies of serpentining vapor. It was another world, and my very sense of equilibrium was disturbed by an evil vertigo as I gazed. It seemed to me that my bed was heaving dizzily, was turning slowly, deliriously toward the gulf; that the feculent vista and the vile apparition were swimming beneath me; that I would fall toward them in another moment and be precipitated forever into that world of abysmal monstrosity and obscenity.

In a start of profound alarm, I fought my vertigo, fought the sense that another will than mine was drawing me, that the unclean gargoyle was luring me by some unspeakable mesmeric spell, as a serpent is said to lure its prey. I seemed to read a nameless purpose in its yellow-slitted eyes, in the soundless moving of its oozy lips; and my very soul recoiled with nausea and revulsion as I breathed its pestilential fetor.

Apparently, the mere effort of mental resistance was enough. The vista and the face receded; they went out in a swirl of daylight. I saw the design of tea roses on the wallpaper beyond; and the bed beneath me was sanely horizontal once more. I lay sweating with my terror, all adrift on a sea of nightmare surmise of unearthly threat and whirlpool madness, till the ringing of the telephone bell recalled me automatically to the known world.

I sprang to answer the call. It was Cyprian, though I should hardly have recognized the dead, hopeless tones of his voice, from which the mad pride and self-assurance of the previous day had wholly vanished.

"I must see you at once," he said. "Can you come to the studio?"

I was about to refuse, to tell him that I had been called home suddenly, that there was no time, that I must catch the noon train — anything to avert the ordeal of another visit to that place of mephitic evil — when I heard his voice again.

"You simply must come, Philip. I can't tell you about it over the phone, but a dreadful thing has happened: Marta had disappeared."

I consented, telling him that I would start for the

studio as soon as I had dressed. The whole nightmare had closed in, had deepened immeasurably with his last words; but remembering the haunted face of the girl, her hysteric fears, her frantic plea and my vague promise, I could not very well decline to go.

I dressed and went out with my mind in a turmoil of abominable conjecture, of ghastly doubt, and apprehension all the more hideous because I was unsure of its object. I tried to imagine what had happened, tried to piece together the frightful, evasive, half-admitted hints of unknown terror into a tangible coherent fabric, but found myself involved in a chaos of shadowy menace.

I could not have eaten any breakfast, even if I had taken the necessary time. I went at once to the studio, and found Cyprian standing aimlessly amid his baleful statuary. His look was that of a man who has been stunned by the blow of some crushing weapon, or has gazed on the very face of Medusa. He greeted me in a vacant manner, with dull, toneless words. Then, like a charged machine, as if his body rather than his mind were speaking, he began at once to pour forth the atrocious narrative.

"They took her," he said, simply. "Maybe you didn't know it, or weren't sure of it; but I've been doing all my new sculptures from life — even that last group. Marta was posing for me this forenoon — only an hour ago — or less. I had hoped to finish her part of the modeling today; and she wouldn't have had to come again for this particular piece. I hadn't called the Things this time, since I knew she was beginning to fear them more and more. I think she feared them on my account more than her own — and they were making me a little uneasy too, by the boldness with which they sometimes lingered when I had ordered then to leave, and the way they would sometimes appear when I didn't want them.

"I was busy with some of the final touches on the girl-figure, and wasn't even looking at Marta, when suddenly I knew that the Things were there. The smell told me, if nothing else — I guess you know what the smell is like. I looked up, and found that the studio was full of them — they had never before appeared in such numbers. They were surrounding Marta, were crowding and jostling each other, were all reaching toward her with their filthy talons; but even then, I didn't think that they could harm her. They aren't material beings, in the sense that we are, and they really have no physical power outside their own plane. All that they do have is a sort of snaky mesmerism, and they'll always try to drag you down to their own dimension by means of it. God help anyone who yields to them; but you don't have to go, unless you are weak, or willing. I've never had any doubt of my power to resist them, and I didn't really dream they could do anything to Marta.

"It startled me, though, when I saw the whole crowding hellpack, and I ordered them to go pretty sharply. I was angry — and somewhat alarmed, too. But they merely grimaced and slavered, with that slow, twisting movement of their lips that is like a voiceless gibbering, and then they closed in on Marta, just as I represented them doing in that accursed group of sculpture. Only there were scores of them now, instead of merely seven.

"I can't describe how it happened, but all at once their foul talons had reached the girl; they were pawing her, were pulling at her hands, her arms, her body. She screamed and I hope I'll never hear another scream so full of black agony and soul-unhinging fright. Then I knew that she had yielded to them — either from choice, or from excess of terror — and knew that they were taking her away.

"For a moment, the studio wasn't there at all — only a long, gray, oozing plain, beneath skies where the fumes of hell were writhing like a million ghostly and distorted dragons. Marta was sinking into that ooze, and the Things were all about her, gathering in fresh hundreds from every side, fighting each other for place, sinking with her like bloated, misshaped fen-creatures into their native slime. Then everything vanished — and I was standing here in the studio, all alone with these damned sculptures."

He paused for a little, and stared with dreary, desolate eyes at the floor. Then:

"It was awful, Philp, and I'll never forgive myself for having anything to do with those monsters. I must have been a little mad, but I've always had a strong ambition to create some real stuff in the field of the grotesque and visionary and macabre. I don't suppose you ever suspected, back in my stodgy phase, that I had a veritable appetence for such things. I wanted to do in sculpture what Poe and Lovecraft and Baudelaire have done in literature, what Rops and Goya did in pictorial art.

"That was what led me into the occult, when I realized my limitations. I knew that I had to see the dwellers of the invisible worlds before I could depict them. I wanted to do it. I longed for this power of vision and representation more than anything else. And then, all at once, I found that I had the power of summoning the unseen. . . .

"There was no magic involved, in the usual sense of the word — no spells and circles, no pentacles and burning gums from old sorcery books. At bottom, it was just will power, I guess — a will to divine the satanic, to summon the innumerable malignities and grotesqueries that people other planes than ours, or mingled unperceived with humanity.

"You've no idea what I have beheld, Philip. These statues of mine — these devils, vampires, lamias, satyrs — were all done from life, or, at least from recent memory. The originals are what the occultists would call elementals, I suppose. There are endless worlds, contiguous to our own, or coexisting with it, that such beings inhabit. All the creations of myth and fantasy, all the familiar spirits that sorcerers have evoked, are resident in these worlds.

"I made myself their master, I levied upon them at will. Then, from a dimension that must be a little lower than all others, a little nearer the ultimate nadir of hell, I called the innominate beings who posed for thie new figure-piece.

"I don't know what they are, but I have surmised a good deal. They are hateful as the worms of the Pit, they are malevolent as harpies, they drool with a poisonous hunger not to be named or imagined. But I believed that they were powerless to do anything outside their own sphere, and I've always laughed at them when they tried to entice me — even though that snakish mental pull of theirs was rather creepy at times. It was as if soft, invisible, gelatinous arms were trying to drag you down from the firm shore into a bottomless bog.

"They are hunters — I am sure of that — the hunters from Beyond. God knows what they will do to Marta now that they have her at their mercy. That vast, viscid, miasma-haunted place to which they took her is awful beyond the imagining of a Satan. Perhaps — even there — they couldn't harm her body. But bodies aren't what they want — it isn't for human flesh that they grope with those ghoulish claws, and gape and slaver with those gangrenous mouths. The brain itself — and the soul, too — is their food: they are the creatures who prey on the minds of madmen and madwomen, who devour the disembodied spirits that have fallen from the cycles of incarnation, have gone down beyond the possibility of rebirth.

"To think of Marta in their power — it is worse than hell or madness. Marta loved me, and I loved her, too, though I didn't have the sense to realize it, wrapped as I was in my dark, baleful ambition and impious egotism. She was afraid for me, and I believe she surrendered voluntarily to the Things. She must have thought that they would leave me alone if they secured another victim in my place."

He ceased, and began to pace idly and feverishly about. I saw that his hollow eyes were alight with torment, as if the mechanical telling of his horrible story had in some manner served to requicken his crushed mind. Utterly and starkly appalled by his hideous revelations, I could say nothing, but could only stand and watch his torture-twisted face.

Incredibly, his expression changed, with a wild, startled look that was instantly transfigured into joy. Turning to follow his gaze, I saw that Marta was standing in the center of the room. She was nude, except for a Spanish shawl that she must have worn while posing. Her face was bloodless as the marble of a tomb, and her eyes were wide and blank, as if she had been drained of all life, of all thought or emotion or memory, as if even the knowledge of horror had been taken away from her. It was the face of the living dead, and the soulless mask of ultimate idiocy; and the joy faded from Cyyrian's eyes as he stepped toward her.

He took her in his arms, he spoke to her with a desperate, loving tenderness, with cajoling and caressing words. She made no answer, however, no movement of recognition or awareness, but stared beyond him with her blank eyes, to which the daylight and the darkness, the void air and her lover's face, would henceforward be the same. He and I both knew, in that instant, that she would never again respond to any human voice, or to human love or terror; that she was like an empty cerement, retaining the outward form of that which the worms have eaten in their mausolean darkness. Of the noisome pits wherein she had been, of that bournless realm and its pullulating phantoms, she could tell us nothing: her agony had ended with the terrible mercy of complete forgetfulness.

Like one who confronts the Gorgon, I was frozen by her wide and sightless gaze. Then, behind her, where stood an array of carven Satans and lamias, the room seemed to recede, the walls and floors dissolved in a seething, unfathomable gulf, amid whose pestilential vapors the statues were mingled in momentary and loathsome ambiguity with the ravening faces, the hunger-contorted forms that swirled toward us from their ultra-dimensional limbo like a devil-laden hurricane from Malebolge. Outlined against that boiling, measureless cauldron of malignant storm, Marta stood like an image of glacial death and silence in the arms of Cyprian. Then, once more, after a little, the abhorrent vision faded, leaving only the diabolic statuary.

I think that I alone had beheld it; that Cyprian had seen nothing but the dead face of Marta. He drew her close, he repeated his hopeless words of tenderness and cajolery. Then, suddenly, he released her with a vehement sob of despair. Turning away, while she stood and still looked on with unseeing eyes, he snatched a heavy sculptor's mallet from the table on which it was lying and proceeded to smash with furious blows the newly-modeled group of gargoyles, till nothing was left but the figure of the terror-maddened girl, crouching above a mass of cloddish fragments and formless, half-dried clay.

THE SATYR

Raoul, Comte de la Frênaie, was by nature the most unsuspicious of husbands. His lack of suspicion, perhaps, was partly lack of imagination; and, for the rest, was doubtless due to the dulling of his observational faculties by the heavy wines of Averoigne. At any rate, he had never seen anything amiss in the friendship of his wife, Adèle, with Olivier du Montoir, a young poet who might in time have rivalled Ronsard as one of the most brilliant luminaries of the Pléiade, if it had not been for an unforeseen but fatal circumstance. Indeed, M. le Comte had been rather proud than otherwise, because of the interest shown in Mme. la Comtesse by this erudite and comely youth, who had already moistened his lips at the fount of Helicon and was becoming known throughout other provinces than Averoigne for his melodious villanelles and graceful ballades. Nor was Raoul disturbed by the fact that many of these same villanelles and ballades were patently written in celebration of Adèle's visible charms, and made liberal mention of her wine-dark tresses, her golden eyes, and sundry other details no less alluring, and equally essential to feminine perfection. M. le Comte did not pretend to understand poetry: like many others, he considered it something apart from all common sense or mundane relevancy; and his mental powers became totally paralysed whenever they were confronted by anything in rhyme and metre. In the meanwhile, the ballades and their author were gradually waxing in boldness.

That year, the snows of an austere winter had melted away in a week of halcyon warmth; and the land was filled with the tender green and chrysolite and chrysoprase of early spring. Olivier came oftener and oftener to the château de la Frênaie, and he and Adèle were often

100

alone, since they had so much to talk that was beyond the interests or the comprehension of M. le Comte. And now, sometimes, they walked abroad in the forest about the château, the forest that rolled a sea of vernal verdure almost to the grey walls and barbican, and within whose sun-warm glades the perfume of the first wild flowers was tingeing delicately the quiet air. If people gossiped, they did so discreetly and beyond hearing of Raoul, or of Adèle and Olivier.

All things being as they were, it is hard to know just why M. le Comte became suddenly troubled concerning the integrity of his marital honour. Perhaps, in some interim of the hunting and drinking between which he divided nearly all his time, he had noticed that his wife was growing younger and fairer and was blooming as a woman never blooms except to the magical sunlight of love. Perhaps he had caught some glance of ardent or affectionate understanding between Adèle and Olivier; or, perhaps, it was the influence of the premature spring, which had pierced the vinous muddlement of his brain with an obscure stirring of forgotten thoughts and emotions, and thus had given him a flash of insight. At any rate, he was troubled when, on this afternoon of earliest April, he returned to the château from Vyones, where he had gone on business, and learned from his servitors that Mme. la Comtesse and Olivier du Montoir had left a few minutes previously for a promenade in the forest. His dull face, however, betrayed little. He seemed to reflect for a moment. Then:

"Which way did they go? I have reason to see Mme. la Comtesse at once."

His servants gave him the required direction, and he went out, following slowly the footpath they had indicated, till he was beyond sight of the château. Then he quickened his pace, and began to finger the hilt of his rapier as he went on through the thickening woods.

"I am a little afraid, Olivier. Shall we go any farther?"

Adèle and Olivier had wandered beyond the limits of their customary stroll, and were nearing a portion of the forest of Averoigne where the trees were older and taller than all others. Here, some of the huge oaks were said to date back to pagan days. Few people ever passed beneath them; and queer beliefs and legends concerning them had been prevalent among the local peasantry for ages. Things had been seen within these precincts, whose very existence was an affront to science and a blasphemy to religion; and evil influences were said to attend those who dared to intrude upon the sullen umbrage of the immemorial glades and thickets. The beliefs varied, and the legends were far from explicit; but all agreed that the wood was haunted by some entity inimical to man, some primordial spirit of ill that was ancienter than Christ or Satan. Panic, madness, demoniac possession, or baleful, unreasoning passions that led them to doom, were the lot of all who had trodden the demesnes of this entity. There were those who whispered what the spirit was, who told incredible tales regarding its true nature, and described its true aspect; but such tales were not meet for the ear of devout Christians.

"Prithee, let us go on," said Olivier. "Look you, Madame, and see how the ancient trees have put on the emerald freshness of April, how innocently they rejoice in the sun's return."

"But the stories people tell, Olivier."

"They are stories to frighten children. Let us go on. There is nothing to harm us here, but much of beauty to enchant."

Indeed, as he had said, the great-limbed oaks and venerable beeches were fresh with their new-born foliage. The forest wore an aspect of blitheness and vertumnal gaiety, and it was hard to believe the old superstitions and legends. The day was one of those days when hearts that feel the urgency of an unavowed love are fain to wander indefinitely. So, after certain feminine demurs, and many reassurances, Adèle allowed Olivier to persuade her, and they went on.

The feet of animals, if not of men, had continued the path they were following, and had made an easy way into the wood of fabulous evil. The drooping boughs enfolded them with arms of soft verdure, and seemed to draw them in; and shafts of yellow sunshine rifted the high trees, to aureole the lovely secret lilies that bloomed about the darkly writhing coils of enormous roots. The trees were twisted and knotted, were heavy with centurial incrustations of bark, were humped and misshapen with the growth of unremembered years; but there was an air of antique wisdom about them, together with a tranquil friendliness. Adèle exclaimed with delight; and neither she nor Olivier was aware of anything sinister or doubtful in the unison of exquisite beauty and gnarled quaintness which the old forest offered to them.

"Was I not right?" Olivier queried. "Is there ought to fear in harmless trees and flowers?"

Adèle smiled, but made no other answer. In the circle of bright sunlight where they were now standing, she and Olivier looked at each other with a new and pervasive intimacy. There was a strange perfume on the windless air, coming in slow wafts from an indiscernible source — a perfume that seemed to speak insidiously of love and languor and amorous yielding. Neither knew the flower from which it issued, for all at once there were many unfamiliar blossoms around their feet, with heavy bells of carnal white or pink, or curled and twining petals, or hearts like a rosy wound. Looking, they saw each other as in a sudden dazzle of flame; and each felt a violent quickening of the blood, as if they had drunk a sovereign philtre. The same thought was manifest in the bold fervour of Olivier's eyes, and the modest flush upon the cheeks of Mme. la Comtesse. The long-cherished love, which neither had openly declared up to this hour, was clamouring importunately in the veins of both. They resumed their onward walk; and both were now silent through the self-same feeling of embarrassment and constraint.

They dared not look at each other; and neither of them had eyes for the changing character of the wood through which they wandered; and neither saw the foul, obscene deformity of the grey boles that gathered on each hand, or the shameful and monstrous fungi that reared their spotted pallor in the shade, or the red, venerous flowers that flaunted themselves in the sun. The spell of their desire was upon the lovers; they were drugged with the mandragora of passion; and everything beyond their own bodies, their own hearts, the throbbing of their own delirious blood, was vaguer than a dream.

The wood grew thicker and the arching boughs above were a weft of manifold gloom. The eyes of ferine animals peered from their hidden burrows, with gleams of crafty crimson or chill, ferocious beryl; and the dank smell of stagnant waters, choked with the leaves of bygone autumn, arose to greet Adèle and Olivier, and to break little the perilous charm that possessed them.

They paused on the edge of a rock-encircled pool, above which the ancient alders twined their decaying tops, as if to maintain forever the mad posture of a superannuate frenzy. And there, between the nether boughs of the alders in a frame of new leaves, they saw the face that leered upon them.

The apparition was incredible; and, for the space of a

long breath, they could not believe they had really seen it.
There were two horns in a matted mass of coarse, animal-
like hair above the semi-human face with its obliquely
slitted eyes and fang-revealing mouth and beard of wild-
boar bristles. The face was old — incomputably old; and
its lines and wrinkles were those of unreckoned years of
lust; and its look was filled with the slow, unceasing
increment of all the malignity and corruption and cruelty
of elder ages. It was the face of Pan, as he glared from his
secret wood upon travellers taken unaware.

Adèle and Olivier were seized by a nightmare terror,
as they recalled the old legends. The charm of their pas-
sionate obsession was broken, and the drug of desire
relinquished its hold on their senses. Like people awak-
ened from a heavy sleep, they saw the face, and heard
through the tumult of their blood the cachinnation of a
wild and evil and panic laughter, as the apparition vanished among the boughs.

Shuddering, Adèle flung herself for the first time
into the arms of her lover.

"Did you see it?" she whispered, as she clung to him.

Olivier drew her close. In that delicious nearness, the
horrible thing he had seen and heard became somehow
improbable and unreal. There must have been a double
sorcery abroad, to lull his horror thus; but he knew not
whether the thing had been a momentary hallucination,
a fantasy wrought by the sun amid the alder-leaves, or
the demon that was fabled to dwell in Averoigne; and the
startlement he had felt was somehow without meaning
or reason. He could even thank the apparition, whatever
it was, because it had thrown Adèle into his embrace. He
could think of nothing now but the proximity of that
warm, delectable mouth, for which he had hungered so
long. He began to reassure her, to make light of her fears,
to pretend that she could have seen nothing; and his reas-

surances merged into ardent protestations of love. He kissed her . . . and they both forgot the vision of the satyr. . . .

They were lying on a patch of golden moss, where the sunrays fell through a single cleft in the high foliage, when Raoul found them. They did not see or hear him, as he paused and stood with drawn rapier before the vision of their unlawful happiness.

He was about to fling himself upon them and impale the two with a single thrust where they lay, when an unlooked-for and scarce conceivable thing occurred. With swiftness veritably supernatural, a brown hairy creature, a being that was not wholly man, not wholly animal, but some hellish mixture of both, sprang from amid the alder branches and snatched Adèle from Olivier's embrace. Olivier and Raoul saw it only in one fleeting glimpse, and neither could have described it clearly afterwards. But the face was that which had leered upon the lovers from the foliage; and the shaggy legs and body were those of a creature of antique legend. It disappeared as incredibly as it had come, bearing the woman in its arms; and her shrieks of terror were surmounted by the pealing of its mad, diabolical laughter.

The shrieks and laughter died away at some distant remove in the green silence of the forest, and were not followed by any other sound. Raoul and Olivier could only stare at each other in complete stupefaction.

THE PASSING OF APHRODITE

In all the lands of Illarion, from mountain-valleys rimmed with un-melting snow, to the great cliffs of sard whose reflex darkens a sleepy, tepid sea, were lit as of old the green and amethyst fires of summer. Spices were on the wind that mountaineers had met in the high glaciers; and the eldest wood of cypress, frowning on a sky-clear bay, was illumined by scarlet orchids. . . . But the heart of the poet Phaniol was an urn of black jade overfraught by love with sodden ashes. And because he wished to forget for a time the mockery of myrtles, Phaniol walked alone in the waste bordering upon Illarion; in a place that great fires had blackened long ago, and which knew not the pine or the violet, the cypress or the myrtle. There, as the day grew old, he came to an unsailed ocean, whose waters were dark and still under the falling sun, and bore not the memorial voices of other seas. And Phaniol paused, and lingered upon the ashen shore; and dreamt awhile of that sea whose name is Oblivion.

Then, from beneath the westering sun, whose bleak light was prone on his forehead, a barge appeared and swiftly drew to the land: albeit there was no wind, and the oars hung idly on the foamless wave. And Phaniol saw that the barge was wrought of ebony fretted with curious anaglyphs, and carved with luxurious forms of gods and beasts, of satyrs and goddesses and women; and the figurehead was a black Eros with full unsmiling mouth and implacable sapphire eyes averted, as if intent upon things not lightly to be named or revealed. Upon the deck of the barge were two women, one pale as the northern moon, and the other swart as equatorial midnight. But both were clad imperially, and bore the mien of goddesses or of those who dwell near to the goddesses. Without word or gesture, they regarded Phaniol; and, marvelling, he inquired, "What seek ye?"

Then, with one voice that was like the voice of hesperian airs among palms at evening twilight in the Fortunate Isles, they answered, saying:

"We wait the goddess Aphrodite, who departs in weariness and sorrow from Marion, and from all the lands of this world of petty loves and pettier mortalities. Thou, because thou art a poet, and hast known the great sovereignty of love, shalt behold her departure. But they, the men of the court, the marketplace and the temple, shall receive no message nor sign of her going-forth, and will scarcely dream that she is gone. . . . Now, O Phaniol, the time, the goddess and the going-forth are at hand."

Even as they ceased, One came across the desert; and her coming was a light on the far hills; and where she trod the lengthening shadows shrunk, and the grey waste put on the purple asphodels and the deep verdure it had worn when those queens were young, that now are a darkening legend and a dust of mummia. Even to the shore she came and stood before Phaniol, while the sunset greatened, filling sky and sea with a flush as of new-blown blossoms, or the inmost rose of that coiling shell which was consecrate to her in old time. Without robe or circlet or garland, crowned and clad only with the sunset, fair with the dreams of man but fairer yet than all dreams: thus she waited, smiling tranquilly, who is life or death, despair or rapture, vision or flesh, to gods and poets and galaxies unknowable. But, filled with a wonder that was also love, or much more than love, the poet could find no greeting.

"Farewell, O Phaniol," she said, and her voice was the sighing of remote waters, the murmur of waters moon-withdrawn, forsaking not without sorrow a proud island tall with palms. "Thou hast known me and worshipped all thy days till now, but the hour of my departure is come: I go, and when I am gone, thou shalt worship still and shalt not know me. For the destinies are thus, and not forever to any man, to any world or to any god, is it given to possess me wholly. Autumn and spring will return when I am past, the one with yellow leaves, the other with yellow violets; birds will haunt the renewing myrtles; and many little loves will be thine. Not again to thee or to any man will return the perfect vision and the perfect flesh of the goddess."

Ending thus, she stepped from that ashen strand to the dark prow of the barge; and even as it had come, without wafture of wind or movement of oar, the barge put out on a sea covered with the fallen fading petals of sunset. Quickly it vanished from view, while the desert lost those ancient asphodels and the deep verdure it had worn again for a little. Darkness, having conquered Illarion, came slow and furtive on the path of Aphrodite; shadows mustered innumerably to the grey hills and the heart of the poet Phaniol was an urn of black jade overfraught by love with sodden ashes.

THE TALE OF
SIR JOHN MAUNDEVILLE

Foreword

This tale was suggested by the reading of *The Voyages and Travels of Sir John Maundeville,* in which the fantastic realm of Abchaz and the darkness-covered province of Hanyson are actually described! I recommend this colourful fourteenth-century book to lovers of fantasy. Sir John even tells, in one chapter, how diamonds propagate themselves! Truly, the world was a wonderful place in those times, when almost everyone believed in the verity of such marvels.

Now in his journeying Sir John Maundeville had passed well to one side of that remarkable province in the kingdom of Abchaz which was called Hanyson; and, unless he was greatly deceived by those of whom he had inquired the way, could deem himself within two days' travel of that neighboring realm of Georgia.

He had seen the river that flowed out from Hanyson, a land of hostile idolators on which there lay the curse of perpetual darkness; and wherein, it was told, the voices of people, the crowing of cocks and the neighing of horses had sometimes been heard by those who approached its confines. But he had not paused to investigate the verity of these marvels; since the direct route of his journey was through another region; and also Hanyson was a place which no man, not even the most hardy, would care to enter without need.

However, as he pursued his wayfaring with the two Armenian Christians who formed his retinue, he began to hear from the inhabitants of that portion of Abchaz the rumor of an equally dread demesne, named Antehar, lying before him on the road to Georgia. The tales they told were both vague and frightful, and were of varying import; some said that this country was a desolation peopled only by the liches of the dead and by loathly phantoms; others, that it was subject to the ghouls and afrits, who devoured the dead and would suffer no living mortal to trespass upon their dominions; and still others spoke of things all too hideous to be described, and of dire necromancies that prevailed even as the might of emperors doth prevail in more usually ordered lands. And the tales agreed only in this, that Antchar had been within mortal memory one of the fairest domains of Abchaz, but had been utterly laid waste by an unknown pestilence, so that its high cities and broad fields were long since abandoned to the desert and to such devils and other creatures as inhabit waste places. And the tellers of the tales agreed in warning Sir John to avoid this region and to take the road which ran deviously to the north of Antchar; for Antchar was a place into which no man had gone in latter times.

The good knight listened gravely to all these, as was his wont; but being a stout Christian, and valorous withal, he would not suffer them to deter him from his purpose. Even when the last inhabited village had been left behind, and he came to the division of the ways, and saw verily that the highway into Antchar had not been trodden by man or beast for generations, he refused to change his intention but rode forward stoutly while the Armenians followed with much protest and trepidation.

Howbeit, he was not blind to the sundry disagreeable tokens that began to declare themselves along the way. There were neither trees, herbs nor lichens anywhere, such as would grow in any wholesome land; but low hills mottled with a leprosy of salt, and ridges bare as the bones of the dead.

Anon he came to a pass where the hills were strait and steep on each hand, with pinnacled cliffs of a dark stone crumbling slowly into dust and taking shapes of wild horror and strangeness, of demonry and Satanry as they crumbled. There were faces in the stone, having the semblance of ghouls or goblins, that appeared to move and twist as the travellers went by; and Sir John and his companions were troubled by the aspect of these faces and the similitudes which they bore to one another. So much alike, indeed, were many of them, that it seemed as if their first exemplars were preceding the wayfarers, to mock them anew at each turn. And aside from those which were like ghouls or goblins, there were others having the features of heathen idols, uncouth and hideous to behold; and others still that were like the worm-gnawed visages of the dead; and these also appeared to repeat themselves on every hand in a doubtful arid wildering fashion.

The Armenians would have turned back, for they swore that the rocks were alive and endowed with motion, in a land where naught else was living; and they sought to dissuade Sir John from his project. But he said merely, "Follow me, an ye will," and rode onward among the rocks and pinnacles.

Now, in the ancient dust of the unused road, they saw the tracks of a creature that was neither man nor any terrestrial beast; and the tracks were of such unwonted shape and number, and were so monstrous withal, that even Sir John was disquieted thereby; and perceiving them, the Armenians murmured more openly than before.

And now, as they pursued their way, the pinnacles of the pass grew tall as giants, and were riven into the likeness of mighty limbs and bodies, some of which were headless and others with heads of Typhoean enormity. And their shadows deepened between the travellers and the sun, to more than the umbrage of shadows cast by rocks. And in the darkest depth of the ravine, Sir John and his followers met a solitary jackal, which fled them not in the manner of its kind but passed them with articulate words, in a voice hollow and sepulchral as that of a demon, bidding them to turn back, since the land before them was an interdicted realm. All were much startled thereat, considering that this was indeed a thing of enchantment, for a jackal to speak thus, and being against nature, was fore-ominous of ill and peril. And the Armenians cried out, saying they would go no further; and when the jackal had passed from sight, they fled after it, spurring their horses like men who were themselves ridden by devils.

Seeing them thus abandon him, Sir John was somewhat wroth; and also he was perturbed by the warning of the jackal; and he liked not the thought of faring alone into Antchar. But, trusting in our Saviour to forfend him against all harmful enchantments and the necromancies of Satan, he rode on among the rocks until he came forth at length from their misshapen shadows; and emerging thus, he saw before him a grey plain that was like the ashes of some dead land under extinguished heavens.

At sight of this region, his heart misgave him sorely, and he misliked it even more than the twisted faces of the rocks and riven forms of the pinnacles. For here the bones of men, of horses and camels, had marked the way with their pitiable whiteness; and the topmost branches of long dead trees arose like supplicative arms from the sand that had sifted upon the older gardens. And here there were ruinous houses, with doors open to the high-drifting desert, and mausoleums sinking slowly in the dunes. And here, as Sir John rode forward, the sky darkened above him, though not with the passage of clouds or the coming of the simoon, but rather with the strange dusk of midmost eclipse, wherein the shadows of himself and his horse were blotted out, and the tombs and houses were wan as phantoms.

Sir John had not ridden much further, when he met a horned viper or cerastes, crawling toilsomely away from Antchar in the deep dust of the road. And the viper spoke as it passed him, saying with a human voice, "Be warned, and go not onward to Antchar, for this is a realm forbidden to all mortal beings except the dead."

Now did Sir John address himself in prayer to God the Highest, and to Jesus Christ our Saviour and all the blessed Saints, knowing surely that he had arrived in a place that was subject to Satanical dominion. And while he prayed, the gloom continued to thicken, till the road before him was half nighted and was no longer easy to discern. And though he would have still ridden on, his charger halted in the gloom and would not respond to the spur, but stood and trembled like one who is smitten with palsy.

Then, from the twilight that was nigh to darkness, there came gigantic figures, muffled and silent and having, as he thought, neither mouths nor eyes beneath the brow-folds of their sable cerements. They uttered no word, nor could Sir John bespeak them in the fear that came upon him; and likewise he was powerless to draw his sword. And they plucked him from his saddle with fleshless hands, and led him away, half swooning at the horror of their touch, on paths that he perceived only with the dim senses of one who goes down into the shadow of death. And he knew not how far they led him nor in what direction; and he heard no sound as he went, other than the screaming of his horse far off, like a soul in mortal dread and agony: for the footfalls of those who had taken him were soundless, and he could not tell if they were phantoms or haply were veritable demons. A coldness blew upon him, but without the whisper or soughing of wind; and the air he breathed was dense with corruption and such odors as may emanate from a broken charnel.

For a time, in the faintness that had come upon him, he saw not the things that were standing beside the way, nor the shrouded shapes that went by in funeral secrecy. Then, recovering his senses a little, he perceived that there were houses about him and the streets of a town, though these were but scantly to be discerned in the night that had fallen without bringing the stars. However, he saw, or deemed, that there were high mansions and broad thoroughfares and markets; and among them, as he went on, a building that bore the appearance of a great palace, with a façade that glimmered vaguely, and domes and turrets half swallowed up by the lowering darkness.

As he neared the façade, Sir John saw that the glimmering came from within and was cast obscurely through open doors and between broad-spaced pillars. Too feeble was the light for torch or cresset, too dim for any lamp; and Sir John marvelled amid his faintness and terror. But when he had drawn closer still, he saw that the strange gleaming was like the phosphor bred by the putrefaction of a charnel.

Beneath the guidance of those who held him helpless, he entered the building. They led him through a stately hall, in whose carven columns and ornate furniture the opulence of kings was manifest; and thence he came into the great audience-room, with a throne of gold and ebony set on a high dais, all of which was illumed by no other light than the glimmering of decay. And the throne was tenanted, not by any human lord or sultan, but a gray, prodigious creature, of height and bulk exceeding those of man, and having in all its over-swollen form the exact similitude of a charnel-worm. And the worm was alone, and except for the worm and Sir John and those beings who had brought him thither, the great chamber was empty as a mausoleum of old days, whose occupants were long since consumed by corruption.

Then, standing there with a horror upon him as no man had ever envisaged, Sir John became aware that the worm was scrutinizing him severely, with little eyes deep-folded in the obscene bloating of its face, and then, with a dreadful and solemn voice, it addressed him, saying:

"I am king of Antchar, by virtue of having conquered and devoured the mortal ruler thereof, as well as all those who were his subjects. Know then that this land is mine and that the intrusion of the living is unlawful and not readily to be condoned. The rashness and folly thou hast shown in thus coming here is verily most egregious; since thou were warned by the people of Abchaz, and warned anew by the jackal and the viper which thou didst meet on the road to Antchar. Thy temerity hath earned a condign punishment. And before I suffer thee to go hence, I decree that thou shalt lie for a term among the dead, and dwell as they dwell, in a dark sepulcher, and learn the manner of their abiding and the things which none should behold with living eyes. Yea, still alive, it shall be thine to descend and remain in the very midst of death and putrefaction, for such length of time as seemeth meet to correct thy folly and punish thy presumption."

Sir John was one of the worthiest knights of Christendom, and his valor was beyond controversy. But when he heard the speech of the throned worm, and the judgement that it passed upon him, his fear became so excessive that once again he was nigh to swooning. And, still in this state, he was taken hence by those who had brought him to the audience-room. And somewhere in the outer darkness, in a place of tombs and graves and cenotaphs beyond the dim town, he was flung into a deep sepulcher of stone, and the brazen door of the sepulcher was closed upon him.

Lying there through the seasonless midnight, Sir John was companioned only by an unseen cadaver and by those ministrants of decay who were not yet wholly done with their appointed task. Himself as one half dead, in the sore extremity of his horror and loathing, he could not tell if it were day or night in Antchar; and in all the term of endless hours that he lay there, he heard no sound, other than the beating of his own heart, which soon became insufferably loud, and oppressed him like the noise and tumult of a great throng.

Appalled by the clamor of his heart, and affrighted by the thing which lay in perpetual silence beside him, and whelmed by the awesomeness and dire necromancy of all that had befallen him, Sir John was prone to despair, and scant was his hope of returning from that imprisonment amid the dead, or of standing once more under the sun as a living man. It was his to learn the voidness of death, to share the abomination of desolation, and to comprehend the unutterable mysteries of corruption; and to do all this not as one who is a mere insensible cadaver, but with soul and body still inseparate. His flesh crept, and his spirit cringed within him, as he felt the crawling of worms that went avidly to the dwindling corpse or came away in glutted slowness. And it seemed to Sir John at that time (and at all times thereafter) that the condition of his sojourn in the tomb was verily to be accounted a worse thing than death.

At last, when many hours or days had gone over

him, leaving the tomb's darkness unchanged by the entrance of any beam or the departure of any shadow, Sir John was aware of a sullen clangor, and knew that the brazen door had been opened. And now, for the first time, by the dimness of twilight that had entered the tomb, he saw in all its piteousness and repulsion the thing with which he had abode so long. In the sickness that fell upon him at this sight, he was haled forth from the sepulcher by those who had thrust him therein; and, fainting once more with the terror of their touch, and shrinking from their gigantic shadowy stature and cerements whose black folds revealed no human visage or form, he was led through Antchar along the road whereby he had come into that dolorous realm.

His guides were silent as before; and the gloom which lay upon the land was even as when he had entered it, and was like the umbrage of some eternal occultation. But at length, in the very place where he had been taken captive, he was left to retrace his own way and to fare alone through the land of ruinous gardens toward the defile of the crumbling rocks.

Weak though he was from his confinement, and all bemazed with the things which had befallen him, he followed the road till the darkness lightened once more and he came forth from its penumbral shadow beneath a pale sun. And somewhere in the waste he met his charger, wandering through the sunken fields that were covered up by the sand; and he mounted the charger and rode hastily away from Antchar through the pass of the strange boulders with mocking forms and faces. And after a time he came once more to the northern road by which travellers commonly went to Georgia; and he was rejoined by the two Armenians, who had waited on the confines of Antchar, praying for his secure deliverance.

Long afterwards, when he had returned from his

wayfaring in the East and among the peoples of remote isles, he told of the kingdom of Abchaz in the book that related to his travels; and also he wrote the reign concerning the province of Hanyson. But he made no mention of Antchar, that kingdom of darkness and decay ruled by the throned worm.

THE LIGHT FROM BEYOND

I t will be said, by nearly all who peruse this narrative, that I must have been mad from the beginning; that even the first of the phenomena related herein as a sensory hallucination betokening some grave disorder. It is possible that I am mad now, at those times when the gulfward-sliding tide of memory sweeps me away; those times when I am lost anew in the tracts of dreadful light and unknown entity that were opened before me by the last phase of my experience. But I was sane at the outset, and I am still sane enough to write down a sober and lucid account of all that occurred.

My solitary habit of life, as well as my reputation for eccentricity and extravagance, will no doubt be urged against me by many, to support the theory of mental unsoundness. Those who are unconventional enough to credit me with rationality will smile at my story and deem that I have forsaken the province of bizarre pictorial art (in which I have achieved a certain eminence) to invade that of super-scientific fiction.

However, if I wished, I could bring forward much corroborative evidence of the strange visitations. Some of the phenomena were remarked by other people in the locality; though I did not know this at the time, owing to my thorough isolation. One or two brief and obscure notices, giving a somewhat commonplace meteoric explanation, appeared shortly afterwards in metropolitan journals, and were reprinted even more briefly and obscurely in scientific gazettes. I shall not quote them here, since to do so would involve a repetition of details which, in themselves, are more or less doubtful and inconclusive.

I am Dorian Wiermoth. My series of illustrative paintings, based on the poems of Poe, will perhaps be familiar to some of my readers.

For a number of reasons, some of which it is needless to mention, I had decided to spend a whole year in the high Sierras. On the shore of a tiny sapphire tarn, in a valley sheltered by hemlocks and granite crags, I had built a rough cabin and had stocked it plentifully with provisions, books, and the materials of my art. For the time being, I was independent of a world whose charms and enchantments were, to say the least, no longer irresistible.

The region possessed, however, other allurements than those of seclusion. Everywhere, in the stark mountain masses and pinnacles, the juniper-studded cliffs, the glacier-moulded sheets of rock, there was a mingling of grandeur and grotesquery that appealed most intimately to my imagination. Though my drawings and paintings were never, in any sense, literal transcriptions of nature, and were often avowedly fantastic, I had made at all times a careful study of natural forms. I realized that the wildest evocations of the unknown are merely, at bottom, recombinations of known shapes and colors, even as the farthest worlds are compositions of elements familiar to terrene chemistry.

Therefore, I found much that was suggestive in this scenery; much that I could interweave with the arabesques of weirdly imaginative designs; or could render more directly, as pure landscape, in a semi-Japanese style with which I was then experimenting.

The place in which I had settled was remote from the state highway, the railroad, and the path of airplanes. My only near neighbors were the mountain crows and jays and chipmunks. Occasionally, in my rambles, I met a fisherman or hunter; but the region was miraculously free of tourists. I began a serene regimen of work and study, which was interrupted by no human agency. The thing that ended my stay so prematurely, came, I am sure, from a sphere that is not mapped by geographers, nor listed by astronomers.

The mystery began, without forewarning or pre-science, on a quiet evening in July, after the scimitar-shaped moon had sheathed itself in the hemlocks. I was sitting in my cabin, reading, for relaxation, a detective story whose title I have since forgotten. The day had been quite warm; there was no wind in that sequestered valley; and the oil lamp was burning steadily between the half-open door and the wide windows.

Then, on the still air, there came a sudden aromatic per- fume that filled the cabin like a flooding wave. It was not the resinous odor of the conifers, but a rich and ever-deepening spice that was wholly exotic to the region — perhaps alien to the Earth. It made me think of myrrh and sandal and incense; and yet it was none of these, but a stranger thing, whose very richness was pure and super-nal as the odors that were said to attend the apparition of the Holy Grail.

Even as I inhaled it, startled, and wondering if I were the victim of some hallucination, I heard a faint music that was somehow allied to the perfume and inseparable from it. The sound, like a breathing of fairy flutes, ethere-ally sweet, thrilling, eldritch, was all about me in the room; and I seemed to hear it in my inmost brain, as one hears the sea whisper in a shell.

I ran to the door, I flung it wide open, and stepped out into the azure-green evening. The perfume was everywhere, it arose before me, like the frankincense of veiled altars, from the tarn and the hemlocks, and it seemed to fall from the stilly burning stars above the Gothic trees and granite walls, to the north. Then, turning eastward, I saw the mysterious light that palpitated and revolved in a fan of broad beams upon the hill.

The light was soft, rather than brilliant, and I knew that it could be neither aurora nor airplane beacon. It was hueless — and yet somehow it seemed to include the intimation of a hundred colors lying beyond the familiar spectrum. The rays were like the spokes of a half-hidden wheel that turned slowly and more slowly, but did not change their position. Their center, or hub, was behind the hill. Presently they became stationary, except for a slight trembling. Against them, I saw the bowed masses of several mighty junipers.

I must have stood there for a long while, gaping and staring like any yokel who beholds a marvel beyond his comprehension. I still breathed the unearthly odor, but the music had grown fainter with the slackening of the wheel of light, and had fallen to a sub-auditory sighing — the suspicion of a murmur far away in some undiscovered world. Implicitly, though perhaps illogically, I connected the sound and the scent with that unexplained luminescence. Whether the wheel was just beyond the junipers, on the craggy hilltop, or a billion miles away in astronomic space, I could not decide; and it did not even occur to me that I could climb the hill and ascertain this particular for myself.

My main emotion was a sort of half-mystic wonder, a dreamy curiosity that did not prompt me to action. Idly I waited, with no clear awareness of the passing of time, till the wheel of rays began once more to revolve slowly. It swiftened, and presently I could no longer distinguish the separate beams. All I could see was a whirling disk, like a moon that spun dizzily but maintained the same position relative to the rocks and junipers. Then, without apparent recession, it grew dim and faded on the sapphire darkness. I heard no longer the remote and flute-like murmur; and the perfume ebbed from the valley like an outgoing tide, leaving but elusive wraiths of its unknown spicery.

My sense of wonder sharpened with the passing of these phenomena; but I could form no conclusion as to their origin. My knowledge of natural science, which was far from extensive, seemed to afford no plausible clue. I felt, with a wild thrilling, half-fearful, half-exultant, that the thing I had witnessed was not to be found in the catalogues compiled by human observers.

The visitation, whatever it was, had left me in a state of profound nervous excitement. Sleep, when it came, was intermittent; and the problematic light, perfume, and melody recurred again and again in my dreams with a singular vividness, as if they had stamped themselves upon my brain with more than the force of normal sensory impressions.

I awoke at earliest dawn, filled with a well-nigh feverish conviction that I must visit the eastern hill immediately and learn if any tangible sign had been left by the agency of the turning beams. After a hasty and half-eaten breakfast, I made the ascent, armed with my drawing-pad and pencils. It was a short climb among over-beetling boulders, sturdy tamaracks, and dwarf oaks that took the form of low-growing bushes.

The hill-top itself comprised an area of several hundred yards, roughly elliptic. It fell gently away toward the east, and ended on two sides in sheerly riven cliffs and jagged scarps. There were patches of soil amid the enormous granite folds and outcroppings; but these patches were bare, except for a few alpine flowers and grasses; and the place was given mainly to a number of gnarled and massive junipers, which had rooted themselves by preference in the solid rock. From the beginning, it had been one of my favorite haunts. I had made many sketches of the mightily mortised junipers, some of which, I verily believe, were more ancient than the famed sequoias, or the cedars of Lebanon.

Surveying the scene with eager eyes in the cloudless morning light, I saw nothing untoward at first. As usual, there were deer-tracks in the basins of friable soil; but apart from these, and my own former footprints, there was no token of any visitor. Somewhat disappointed, I began to think that the luminous, turning wheel had been far-off in space, beyond the hill.

Then, wandering on toward the lamer levels of the crest, I found, in a sheltered spot, the thing that had previously been hidden from my view by the trees and outcroppings. It was a cairn of granite fragments — but a cairn such as I had never beheld in all my mountain explorations. Built in the unmistakable form of a star with five blunt angles, it rose waist-high from the middle of a plot of intersifting loam and sand. About it grew a few plants of mountain phlox. On one side were the charred remnants of a tree that had been destroyed by lightning in recent years. On two other sides, forming a right angle, were high walls to which several junipers clung like coiling dragons with tenacious claws, embedded in the riven rock.

On the summit of the strange pile, in the center, I perceived a pale and coldly shining stone with star-like points that duplicated and followed the five angles. This stone, I thought, had been shaped by artificial means. I did not recognize its material; and I felt sure that it was nothing native to the region.

I felt the elation of a discoverer, deeming that I had stumbled on the proof of some alien mystery. The cairn, whatever its purpose, whoever its builders, had been reared during the night; for I had visited this very spot on the previous afternoon, a little before sunset, and would have seen the structure if it had been there at that time.

Somehow, I dismissed immediately and forever all

idea of human agency. There occurred to me the bizarre thought that voyagers from some foreign world had paused on the hill and had left that enigmatic pile as a sign of their visit. In this manner, the queer nocturnal manifestations were accounted for, even if not fully explained.

Arrested by the weird enigma of it all, I had paused on the verge of the loamy basin, at a distance of perhaps twelve feet from the cairn itself. Now, my brain on fire with fantastical surmise, I stepped forward to examine the cairn more closely. To my utter dumfoundment, it appeared to recede before me, preserving the same interval, as I went toward it. Pace after pace I took, but the ground flowed forward beneath me like a treadmill; my moving feet descended in their former tracks; and I was unable to make the least progress toward the goal that was apparently so near at hand! My movements were in no sense impeded, but I felt a growing giddiness, that soon verged upon nausea.

My disconcertment can more readily be imagined than expressed. It seemed obvious that either I or nature had gone suddenly mad. The thing was absurd, impossible — it belied the most elementary laws of dimension. By some incalculable means, a new and arcanic property had been introduced into the space about the cairn.

To test further the presence of this hypothetical property, I abandoned my effort at direct approach, and began to circle the basin, resuming the attempt from other angles. The pile, I found, was equally unapproachable from all sides: at a distance of twelve feet, the soil began its uncanny treadmill movement when I tried to encroach upon it. The cairn, to all intents and purposes, might have been a million miles away, in the gulf between the worlds!

After a while, I gave up my weird and futile experiments, and sat down beneath one of the overhanging junipers. The mystery maddened me, it induced a sort of mental vertigo as I pondered it. But also, it brought into the familiar order of things the exhilaration of a novel and perhaps supernatural element. It spoke of the veiled infinitudes I had vainly longed to explore; it goaded my feverish fantasy to ungovernable flights.

Recalling myself from such conjectures, I studied with sedulous care the stellar pile and the soil around it. Surely the beings who had built it would have left their footprints. However, there were no discernible marks of any kind; and I could learn nothing from the arrangement of the stones, which had been piled with impeccable neatness and symmetry. I was still baffled by the five-pointed object on the summit, for I could recall no terrene mineral that resembled its substance very closely. It was too opaque for moonstone or crystal, too lucid and brilliant for alabaster.

Meanwhile, as I continued to sit there, I was visited by an evanescent whiff of the spicy perfume that had flooded my cabin on the previous night. It came and went like a dying phantom, and I was never quite sure of its presence.

At length I roused myself and made a thorough search of the hill-top, to learn if any other trace had been left by the problematic visitors. In one of the sandy patches of soil, near the northern verge, I saw a curious indentation, like the slender, three-toed footmark of some impossibly gigantic bird.

Close at hand was the small hollow from which a loose fragment of stone, doubtless employed in the building of the cairn, had been removed. The three-pointed mark was very faint, as if the maker had trodden there with an airy lightness. But apart from the finding of this doubtful vestige, my search was wholly without result.

II: The Mystery Deepens

During the weeks that ensued, the unearthly riddle upon which I had fallen preoccupied me almost to the point of mania. Perhaps, if there had been anyone with whom I could have discussed it, anyone who could have thrown upon it the calm and sober light of technical knowledge, I might have rid myself of the obsession to some extent. But I was entirely alone; and, to the best of my belief, the neighborhood of the cairn was visited by no other human being at that time.

On several occasions, I renewed my efforts to approach the cairn; but the unheard-of, incredible property of a concealed extension, a treadmill flowing, still inhered, in the space about it, as if established there to guard it from all intrusion. Faced with this abrogation of known geometry, I felt the delirious horror of one for whom the infinite has declared its yawning gulf amid the supposed solidity of finite things.

I made a pencil drawing of the long, light footmark before it was erased by the Sierran winds; and from that one vestige, like a paleontologist who builds up some prediluvian monster from a single bone, I tried to reconstruct in my imagination the being that had left it there. The cairn itself was the theme of numerous sketches; and I believe that I formed and debated in turn almost every conceivable theory as to its purpose and the identity of its builders.

Was it a monument that marked the grave of some intercosmic voyager from Algol or Aldebaran? Had it been reared as a token of discovery and possession by a Columbus of Achernar, landing on our planet? Did it indicate the site of a mysterious cache, to which the makers would return at some future time? Was it a land-mark between dimensions? a hieroglyphic milepost? a signal for the guidance of other travelers who might pass among the worlds, going from deep to deep?

All conjectures were equally valid — and worthless. Before the wildering mystery of it all, my human igno-rance drove me to veritable frenzy.

A fortnight had gone by, and the midsummer month was drawing to its close, when I began to notice certain new phenomena. I have mentioned, I think, that there were a few tiny patches of alpine phlox within the circle of occultly altered space around the cairn. One day, with a startlement that amounted to actual shock, I saw that an extraordinary change had occurred in their pale blos-soms. The petals had doubled in number, they were now of abnormal size and heaviness, and were tinged with ardent purple and lambent ruby. Perhaps the change had been going on for some time without my perception; per-haps it had developed overnight. At any rate, the modest little flowers had taken on the splendor of asphodels from some mythologic land!

Beyond all mortal trespass, they flamed in that en-chanted area, moated with unseen immensities. Day after day I returned, smitten with the awe of one who witnesses a miracle, and saw them there, ever larger and brighter, as if they were fed by other elements than the known air and earth.

Then, presently, in the berries of a great juniper bough that overhung the ring, I perceived a correspond-ing change. The tiny, dull-blue globes had enlarged enor-mously, and were colored with a lucent crimson, like the fiery apples of some exotic paradise. At the same time, the foliage of the bough brightened to a tropic verdancy. But on the main portion of the tree, outside the cryptic circle, the leaves and berries were unaltered.

It was as if something of another world had been intercalated with ours . . . More and more, I began to feel that the star of lucent, nameless stone that topped the cairn was in some manner of source or key of these unique phenomena. But I could prove nothing, could learn nothing. I could feel sure of only one thing: I was witnessing the action of forces that had never intruded heretofore upon human observation. These forces were obedient to their own laws -which, it appeared, were not altogether synonymous with the laws that man in his presumption has laid down for the workings of nature. The meaning of it all was a secret told in some alien, key-less cipher.

I have forgotten the exact date of those final occurrences, in whose aftermath I was carried beyond the imaginable confines of time and space. Indeed, it seems to me that it would be impossible to date them in terms of terrene chronology. Sometimes I feel that they belong only to the cycles of another world; sometimes, that they never happened; sometimes, that they are still happening — or yet to happen.

I remember, though, that there was a half-moon above the crags and firs on that fatal evening. The air had turned sharp with a prescience of the coming autumn, and I had closed the door and windows and had kindled a fire of dead juniper-wood that was perfuming the cabin with its subtle incense. I heard the soughing of a wind in the higher hemlocks, as I sat before my table, looking over the recent sketches I had made of the cairn and its surroundings, and wondering for perhaps the millionth time if I, or anyone, would ever solve the unearthly riddle.

This time, I began to hear the faint, aerial music, as if in the inmost convolutions of my brain, before I caught the mystic odor. At first, it was little more than the memory of a sound; but it seemed to rise and flow and pour outward, slowly, tortuously, as if through the windings of some immeasurable conch. till it was all about me with its labyrinthine murmuring. The cabin — the world outside — the very heavens — were filled with tenuous horns and flutes that told the incommunicable dreams of a lost elfland.

Then, above the redolence of the clearly burning, smokeless wood, I smelt that other perfume, rich and ethereal, and no less pervasive than on the former occasion. It seemed that the closed doors and windows were no barrier to its advent: it came as if through another medium than the air, another avenue than the space in which we move and have our being.

In a fever of exalted wonder and curiosity, I threw the door open and went out into the sea of unearthly fragrance and melody that overflowed the world. On the eastern hill, as I had expected, the turning wheel of light was slowing in a stationary position beyond the tower-like junipers. The rays were soft and hueless, as before, but their luster was not diminished by the moon.

This time, I felt an imperative desire to solve the enigma of that visitation: a desire that drew me, stumbling and racing upward among the craggy boulders and low-grown bushes. The music ebbed to a far, faint whisper, the wheel revolved more gradually, as I neared the summit.

A rudiment of that caution which humanity has always felt in the presence of unknown things, impelled me to slacken my reckless pace. Several immense trees and granite outcroppings, however, still intervened betwixt myself and the source of those trembling beams. I stole forward, seeing with an inexpressible thrill, as of some mystic confirmation, that the beams emanated from the site of the stelliform cairn.

It was an easy matter to climb the massive folds of rock and reach a vantage from which I could look directly down on that mysterious area. Crawling flat on my stomach, in a line with the mightiest of the over jutting junipers, I attained my objective, and could peer from behind a heavy bough that grew horizontally along the rock; at the wall's edge. The loamy basin in which the cairn had been reared was beneath me. Poised in mid-air, level and motionless, and a little to one side of the cairn, there hung a singular vessel that I can liken only to a great open barge with upward curving prow and stern. In its center, above the bulwarks, arose a short mast or slender pillar, topped with a fiery, dazzling disk from which the wheel of beams, as if from a hub, poured vertically and transversely. The whole vessel was made of some highly translucent material, for I could see the dim outlines of the landscape beyond it: and the beams poured earthward through its bottom with little diminution of their radiance. The disk, as well as I could tell from the sharply foreshortened position in which I viewed the barge, was the only semblance of mechanism.

It was as if a crescent moon of milky crystal had come down to flood that shadowy nook with its alien light. And the prow of this moon was no more than six or seven feet from the granite wall that formed my place of vantage!

Four beings, whom I can compare to no earthly creatures, were hovering in the air about the cairn, without wings or other palpable support, as if they, like the barge, were independent of terrene gravity. Though little less in stature than men, their whole aspect was slight and imponderable to a degree that is found only in birds or insects. Their bodily plasm was almost diaphanous, with its intricate nerves and veinings dimly visible, like iridescent threads through a gauzy fabric of pearl and faint rose.

One of them, hanging aloft before the wheel of beams, with his head averted from my view, was holding in his long, frail hands the cold and lucent star that had topped the cairn. The others, stooping airily, were lifting and throwing aside the fragments that had been piled with such impeccable symmetry.

The faces of two were wholly hidden; but the third presented a strange profile, slightly resembling the beak and eye of an owl beneath an earless cranium that rose to a lofty ridge aigretted with nodding tassels like the top-knot of a quail.

The tearing-down of the pile was accomplished with remarkable deftness and speed; and it seemed that the pipy arms of these creatures were far stronger than one would have imagined. During the process of demolition, they stooped lower and lower, till they floated almost horizontally, just above the ground. Soon all the fragments were removed; and the entities began to scoop away with their fingers the soil beneath, whose looseness appeared to evince a previous digging at some recent date.

Breathless and awed before the cryptic vision, I bent forward from my eyrie, wondering what inconceivable treasure, what cache of unguessed glory and mystery, was about to be exhumed by these otherworld explorers.

Finally, from the deep hollow they had made in the loamy soil, one of the beings withdrew his hand, holding aloft a small and colorless object. Apparently it was the thing for which they had been searching, for the creatures abandoned their delving, and all four of them swam upward toward the barge as if wafted by invisible wings. Two of them took their stations in the rear part of the vessel, standing behind the mast-like pillar and its wheel of rays. The one who bore the shining, star-shaped stone, and the carrier of the dull, unknown object, posted themselves in the prow, at a distance of no more than nine or ten feet from the crag on which I crouched.

For the first time, I beheld their faces in front view, peering straight toward me with glowing, pale-gold eyes of inscrutable strangeness. Whether or not they saw me, I have never been sure: they seemed to gaze through me and beyond — illimitably beyond — into occulted gulfs, and upon worlds forever sealed to the sight of man.

I discerned more clearly now, in the fingers of the foremost being, the nameless object they had dug from beneath the dismantled cairn. It was smooth, drab, oval, and about the size of a falcon's egg. I might have deemed it no more than a common pebble, aside from one peculiar circumstance: a crack in the larger end, from which issued several short, luminous filaments. Somehow, the thing reminded me of a riven seed with sprouting roots.

Heedless of any possible peril, I had risen to my feet and staring raptly at the barge and its occupants. After a few moments. I became aware that the wheel of beams had begun to turn gradually, as if in response to an unperceived mechanism. At the same time, I heard the eerie whispering of a million flutes, I breathed a rushing gale of Edenic spices. Faster and faster the rays revolved, sweeping the ground and the air with their phantom spokes, till I saw only a spinning moon that divided the crescent vessel and seemed to cleave asunder the very earth and rocks.

My senses reeled with the dizzy radiance, the ever-pouring music and perfume. An indescribable sickness mounted through all my being, the solid granite seemed to turn and pitch under my feet like a drunken world, and the heavily buttressed junipers tossed about me against the overturning heavens.

Very swiftly, the wheel, the vessel and its occupants took on a filmy dimness, fading in a manner that is hard to convey, as if, without apparent diminishment of perspective, they were receding into some ultra-geometric space. Their outlines were still before me — and yet they were immeasurably distant. Coincidentally, I felt a terrific suction, an unseen current more powerful than cataracting waters, that seized me as I stood leaning forward from the rock, and swept me past the violently threshing boughs.

I did not fall toward the ground beneath — for there was no longer any ground. With the sensation of being wrenched asunder in the ruin of worlds that had returned to chaos, I plunged into gray and frigid space, that included neither air, earth, stars nor heaven; void, uncreated space, through which the phantom crescent of the strange vessel fell away beneath me, bearing a ghostly moon.

As well as I can recollect, there was no total loss of consciousness at any time during my fall; but, toward the end, there was an increasing numbness, a great dubiety, and a dim perception of enormous arabesques of color that had risen before me, as if created from the gray nothing.

All was misty and two-dimensional, as if this new-made world had not yet acquired the attribute of depth. I seemed to pass obliquely over painted labyrinths. At length, amid soft opals and azures, I came to a winding area of rosy light, and settled into it till the rosiness was all about me.

My numbness gave way to a sharp and painful tingling as of frost-bite, accompanied by a revival of all my senses. I felt a firm grasp about my shoulders, and knew that my head and upper body had emerged from the rosiness.

III: The Infinite World

For an instant, I thought that I was leaning horizontally from a slowly plunging cataract of some occult element, neither water, air nor flame, but somehow analogous to all three. It was more tangible than air, but there was no feeling of wetness; it flowed with the soft fluttering of fire, but it did not burn.

Two of the strange, ethereal entities were drawing me out on a luminous golden cliff, from which an airy vegetation, hued as with the rainbows of towering fountains, projected its lightly arching masses into a gold-green abyss. The crescent barge and its wheel of beams, now stationary, were hovering close at hand in a semi-capsized position. Farther away, beyond the delicate trees, I saw the jutting of horizontal towers. Five suns, drowning in their own glory, were suspended at wide intervals in the gulf.

I wondered at the weird inversion of gravity that my position evinced; and then, as if through a normalizing of equilibrium, I saw that the great cliff was really a level plain, and the cataract a gentle stream.

Now I was standing on the shore, with the people of the barge beside me. They were no longer supporting me with their frail, firm hands. I could not guess their attitude, and my brain awoke with a keen electric shock to the eerie terror and wildering strangeness of it all. Surely the world about me was no part of the known cosmos! The very soil beneath me thrilled and throbbed with unnamable energies. All things, it seemed, were composed of a range of elements nearer to pure force than to common matter. The trees were like fountains of supernal pyrotechnics, arrested and made permanent in mid-air. The structures that soared at far intervals, like celestial minarets, were built as of moulded morning cloud and luminescence. I breathed an air that was more intoxicating than the air of alpine heights.

Out of this world of marvel, I saw the gathering of many people similar to the entities beside me. Amid the trees and towers, from the shimmering vistas, they came as if summoned by magic. Their movements were swift and silent as the gliding of phantoms, and they seemed to tread the air rather than the ground. I could not hear even the least whispering among them, but I had the feeling of inaudible converse all about me — the vibrant thrilling of overtones too high for the human ear.

Their eyes of pale gold regarded me with unsearchable intentness. I noted their softly curving mouths, which appeared to express an alien sadness, but perhaps were not sad at all. Beneath their gaze, I felt a queer embarrassment, followed quickly by something that I can describe only as an inward illumination. This illumination did not seem to be telepathic: it was merely as if my mind had acquired, as a concomitant of the new existence into which I had fallen, a higher faculty or comprehension impossible in its normal state. This faculty was something that I drew in from the strange soil and air, the presence of the strange multitude. Even then, my understanding was only partial, and I knew there was much that still eluded me through certain insuperable limitations of my brain.

The beings, I thought, were benignantly disposed, but were somewhat puzzled as to what should be done with me. Inadvertently, in a way without parallel, I had trespassed upon another cosmos than my own. Caught in the pull of some transdimensional vortex wrought by the crescent vessel as it departed from earth, I had followed the vessel to its own world, which adjoined ours in transcendental space.

This much I understood, but the mechanics of my

entrance into the supernal realm were somewhat obscure to me. Apparently my fall into the rosy river had been providential, for the stream had revived me with its superaqueous element, and had perhaps served to prevent a sort of frostbite that would otherwise have been incurred by my plunge through an interspatial vacuum.

The purpose of the granite cairn, and the visits made by its builders to earth, were things that I could apprehend but dimly. Something had been planted beneath the cairn, and had been left there for a stated interval, as if to absorb from the grosser mundane soil certain elements or virtues lacking in the soil of this ethereal world. The whole process was based on the findings of an arcanic but severely ordered science; and the experiment was one that had been made before. The lucent stone on the cairn, in some way that I could not grasp, had established around it the guarding zone of fluent treadmill space, on which no earthly denizen could intrude. The earthly changes of the vegetation within this zone were due to certain mystic emanations from the planted seed.

The nature of the seed eluded me; but I knew that it possessed an enormous and vital importance. And the time for its transplanting to the otherworld soil was now at hand. My eyes were drawn to the fingers of the entity who carried it, and I saw that the seed had swollen visibly, that the shining rootlets had lengthened from its riven end.

More and more of the people had gathered, lining the shore of that rosy river, and the intervals of the airy boskage, in silent multitude. Some, I perceived, were thin and languid as wasting specters; and their bodily plasm, as if clouded by illness, was dull and opaque, or displayed unhealthy mottlings of shadow amid the semi-translucence that was plainly a normal attribute.

In a clear area, beside the hovering vessel, a hole had

been dug in that Edenic soil. Amid the bewildering flux of my impressions, I had not noticed it heretofore. Now it assumed a momentous import, as the bearer of the seed went forward to deposit his charge in that shallow pit, and bury it with a curious oval spade of crystalline metal beneath the golden element that was like a mixture of loam and sunset glory.

The crowd had drawn back, leaving a vacant field about the planted seed. There was a sense of awful and solemn, ceremonial expectation in the stillness of that waiting people. Dim, sublime, ungraspable images hovered upon the horizon of my thought like unborn suns; and I trembled with the nearness of some tremendous thaumaturgy. But the purpose of it all was still beyond my comprehension.

Darkly I felt the anticipation of the alien throng . . . and somewhere — in myself or in those about me — a great need and a crying hunger that I could not name.

It seemed that whole months and seasons went by; that the five suns revolved about us in altered ecliptics, ere the end of the interim of waiting . . . But time and its passing were perhaps obedient to unknown laws, like all else in that other sphere, and were not as the hours and seasons of earthly time.

There came at last the awaited miracle: the pushing of a pale shoot from the golden sod. Visibly, dynamically it grew, as if fed with the sap of accelerating years that had turned to mere minutes. From it, there burst a multitude of scions, budding in their turn with irised leafage. The thing was a fountain of unsealed glories, an upward-rushing geyser of emerald and opal that took the form of a tree.

The rate of growth was beyond belief, it was like a legerdemain of gods. From moment to moment the boughs multiplied and lengthened with the leaping of wind wrought flames. The foliage spread like a blown spray of jewels. The plant became colossal, it towered with a pillar-thick stem, and its leafage meshed the five suns, and drooped down toward the river and above the barge, the crowd, and the lesser vegetation.

Still the tree grew, and its boughs came down in glorious arches and festoons, laden with starlike blossoms. I beheld the faces of those about me in a soft umbrage, along arboreal arcades, as if beneath some paradisiacal banyan. Then, as the festoons hung nearer, I saw the fruiting of the tree: the small globules, formed as of blood and light, that were left by the sudden withering of the starry blossoms. Swiftly they swelled, attaining the size of pears, and descending till they grew well within my reach — and within the reach of that embowered throng.

It seemed that the marvellous growth had attained its culmination, and was now quiescent. We were domed as if by some fabulous Tree of Life that had sprung from the mated energies of Earth and the celestial Otherworld.

Suddenly I knew the purpose of it all, when I saw that some of the people about me were plucking and devouring the fruit. Many others abstained, however, and I perceived that the sanguine-colored pears were eaten only by the languid, sickly beings I have mentioned before. It seemed that the fruit was a sovereign curative for their illness: even as they devoured it, their bodies brightened, the mottlings of shadow disappeared, and they began to assume the normal aspect of their fellows.

I watched them — and upon me there came a kindred hunger, a profound and mystic craving, together with the reckless vertigo of one who is lost in a world too far and high for human tread. There were doubts that woke within me, but I forgot them even as they woke. There were hands that reached out as if to warn and restrain me, but I disregarded them. One of the luscious, glowing pears hung close before me — and I plucked it.

The thing filled my fingers with a sharp, electric tingling, followed by a coolness that I can compare only to snow beneath a summer sun. It was not formed of anything that we know as matter — and yet it was firm and solid to the touch, and it yielded a winy juice, an ambrosial pulp, between my teeth. I devoured it avidly, and a high, divine elation coursed like a golden lightning through all my nerves and fibers.

I have forgotten much of the delirium (if delirium it was) that ensued . . . There were things too vast for memory to retain. And much that I remember could be told only in the language of Olympus.

I recall, however, the colossal expansion of all my senses, the flowering of thought into stars and worlds, as if my consciousness had towered above its mortal tenement with more than the thaumaturgic spreading of the Tree. It seemed that the life of the strange people had become a province of my being, that I knew from all time the arcana of their wisdom, the preterhuman scale of their raptures and sorrows, of their triumphs and disasters.

Holding all this as an appanage. I rose into spheres ulterior and superior. Infinities were laid before me, I conned them as one cons an unrolled map. I peered down upon the utmost heavens, and the hells that lie contiguous to the heavens; and I saw the perennial process of their fiery transmutation and interchange.

I possessed a million eyes and ears; my nerves were lengthened into nether gulfs, were spun out beyond the suns. I was the master of strange senses, that were posted to oversee the activities of unlit stars and blind planets.

All this I beheld and comprehended with the exultation of a drunken demiurge; and all was familiar to me, as if I had seen it in other cycles.

Then, quickly and terribly, there came the sense of division, the feeling that part of myself no longer shared this empire of cosmic immensitude and glory. My delirium shrank like a broken bubble, and I seemed to lose and leave behind me the colossal, shadowy god that still towered above the stars. I was standing again beneath the Tree, with the transdimensional people about me, and the ruddy fruit still burning in the far-flung arches of leafage.

Here, also, the inexorable doom of division pursued me, and I was no longer one, but two. Distinctly I saw myself, my body and features touched with the ethereal radiance of the beings who were native to that world; but I, who beheld that alter ego, was aware of a dark and iron weight, as if some grosser gravity had claimed me. It seemed that the golden soil was yielding under me like a floor of sunset cloud, and I was plunging and falling through nether emptiness, while that other self remained beneath the Tree.

I awoke with the sultry beams of the midday sun upon my face. The loamy ground on which I lay, the scattered fragments of the cairn beside me, and the rocks and junipers, were irrecognizable as if they had belonged to some other planet than ours. I could not remember them for a long while; and the things I have detailed in this narrative came back to me very tardily, in a broken and disordered sequence.

The manner of my return to Earth is still a mystery. Sometimes I think that the supernal people brought me back in that shining vessel whose mechanism I have never understood. Sometimes, when the madness is upon me, I think that I — or part of myself — was precipitated hither as an aftermath of the eating of the Fruit. The energies to whose operation I exposed myself by that act were wholly incalculable. Perhaps, in accord with the laws of a transdimensional chemistry, there was a partial revibration, and an actual separation of the elements of my body, by which I became two persons, in different worlds. No doubt the physicists will laugh at such ideas . . .

There were no corporeal ill effects from my experience, apart from a minor degree of what appeared to be frostbite, and a curious burning of the skin, mild rather than severe, that might have resulted from a temporary exposure to radioactive matters. But in all other senses, I was, and still am, a mere remnant of my former self . . . Among other things, I soon found that my artistic abilities had deserted me; and they have not returned after an interim of months. Some higher essence, it would seem, has departed wholly and forever.

I have become as it were, a clod. But often, to that clod, the infinite spheres descend in their terror and marvel. I have left the lonely Sierras and have sought the refuge of human nearness. But the streets yawn with uncharted abysms, and Powers unsuspected by others move for me amid the crowd. Sometimes I am no longer here among my fellows, but am standing with the eaters of the fruit, beneath the Tree, in that mystic otherworld.